Koya DeLaney and the Good Girl Blues

Eloise Greenfield

AN **APPLE** PAPERBACK

SCHOLASTIC INC.
New York Toronto London Auckland Sydney

ISBN 0-590-43299-0
ISBN 0-590-29133-5 (meets NASTA specifications)

36 35 40 14 15 16/0

Printed in the U.S.A.

One

Koya felt the laughter coming and knew she wouldn't be able to stop it.

"Mmmp-*hmmmp*!" The first notes slipped through her closed lips.

Cortee, sitting at the desk in front of hers, heard her, looked back and grinned, then nudged Angie, who nudged somebody else, who nudged somebody else, who nudged somebody else. And one by one, they turned away from the lesson Ms. Thomason was teaching.

They watched Koya, all of them smiling and waiting for what they knew was to come — one of Koya's laughing fits.

Koya pressed her lips together, clapped her hand over her mouth, and shook her head, trying hard to hold back the laughter. But she couldn't. She gave in and let the sounds spill, helter-skelter, into the room, slapping her desk four or five times, fast, as if it were responsible for her predicament. Then, the whole sixth-grade class, and Ms. Thomason, too, laughed until their tears rolled. And of them all, only Koya really knew what had been so funny.

It had begun, as always, in her imagination. At first, she had been paying close attention to the lesson. It was about the American Revolution, and Koya loved watching her teacher talk about long-ago events as if they had just happened the day before. Ms. Thomason walked around the room, looking intently into their faces, talking excitedly, as if she were telling friends about something she had seen. She always wore swirly dresses with large splashes of bright colors that looked dramatic against her dark skin.

". . . and so the British soldiers were on their way to Lexington," she had been saying, throwing out her arms, so that her long, loose sleeves flowed. "And the men of the militia were there, and the minutemen came to fight . . ."

Contee raised his hand, as if he had a medical emergency. Everything was urgent with Contee. "Ms. Thomason!" he called. "Ms. Thomason! Why'd they call 'em minutemen?"

"Does anybody have any ideas about that?" Ms. Thomason asked the class. But Koya didn't hear their answers because her imagination had begun to play its usual tricks. In her mind, she saw hundreds of clock hands — minute hands wearing the faces of men, leaving their clocks and marching off to war.

Out of the doors of hundreds of houses they came, rifles on their skinny shoulders, marching to the sound of bass drums. *Da-boom, da-boom, da-boom, da-boom!* They looked so funny. Koya had felt a sudden small giggle in her throat, and when she tried to hold it in, it grew and fought all the harder to escape, until it finally won.

Now, the laughter in the classroom was subsiding, and Ms. Thomason moved to the front of the room, where she stood very still, waiting to get the attention of the class. And in a few moments, they settled down for the last half hour of the school day.

When the bell rang, the class was in the middle of a hot argument about war, whether it was right or wrong. Koya almost didn't want to go home, but Ms. Thomason promised that they would continue the discussion first thing tomorrow, instead of doing arithmetic, and that was more than all right with Koya.

While she was getting her books out of her

desk, Contee and Angie came over to talk. Behind them, Koya's best friend, Dawn, waved at Koya over Contee's shoulder.

"See you in the gym," Dawn said as she left.

"Okay, in a minute," Koya said.

"Koya!" Contee tapped her arm, in a hurry to get her attention. "What was so funny?" he asked. He was squinting a little, trying to make his eyes smaller. He was always being teased for having large eyes.

"Funny? What do you mean?" Koya said. She knew she wasn't going to tell. She never told, no matter how much her classmates begged. She knew that after the big laugh they'd had, nothing she said would be as funny as it had been in her imagination.

"Come on, tell us," Angie said, looking up at Koya. Angie looked too little to be in the sixth grade, and her big puff of hair, held in a rubber band on top of her head, made her narrow face look even smaller. Her voice was as small as she was. "Just this one time. What were you laughing about?"

"Me? Laughing?" Koya asked, with a straight face. "You musta been dreaming."

"Oh, right," Contee said. "I guess me and Angie had the same dream."

"Hey, you slept through the whole Revolutionary War," Koya said. "You were snoring so loud, Ms. Thomason almost jumped out of her skin. She thought it was a cannon going off."

"Yeah, okay," Contee said. "If that's the way you want to be." He and Angie walked away pretending to be mad, then looked back and laughed.

"See you tomorrow, Koya," Angie said, and Koya waved.

Then she went to help Ms. Thomason water the plants, and by the time she got to the gym, Dawn and the other members of the double-dutch team, all from the two sixth-grade classes, had changed into their dark-blue shorts and T-shirts and were ready to start practice. All except Loritha. Koya knew her sister would be the last one ready. She did everything slow, except read and jump double-dutch.

Ms. Harris, the gym teacher, stood with the girls near the two ropes that were laid in straight lines, side by side, on the floor. Koya looked at her, but couldn't read her mood. Her plump face showed no expression as she looked up at the large clock on the wall. Then Loritha came in from the locker room, halfway running, her short, beaded braids shaking as she ran.

"I'm sorry," she said to Ms. Harris.

She gave a quick "hello" look to Koya, sitting alone in the third row of the stands, and joined the other girls down on the floor. She was the youngest member of the team, since she had skipped a grade, but she was the fastest jumper.

Ms. Harris didn't answer Loritha. "Come *on*," she said to all of the girls. "Let's get *started.*"

As soon as she spoke, Koya knew that she was in one of her bad moods. She was batting some of her words through lips that were barely open.

Two girls picked up the ropes, one in each hand. They waited for Ms. Harris to blow the whistle, then began to turn the ropes toward each other, alternating left hand, right hand, left hand, right hand. Two other girls jumped in, one behind the other, while Loritha, Dawn, and the last two girls watched.

Koya watched, too, trying, as always, to see how anybody could do what they did. But they moved much too fast for her to follow their movements. Even the substitutes, performing now, were great. Turning the ropes so fast they were almost a blur. Doing somersaults and flips in the ropes without tripping. Burning up the floor, stomping, stomping in rhythm. Jumping so long and so fast that Koya knew she would have collapsed on the floor long before Ms. Harris blew the whistle to tell them it was time to stop.

"*Disgraceful!*" Ms. Harris said as soon as

the girls stopped jumping. "You are *not* going to be ready for this competition. Do you *want* to be in it or not?"

The girls mumbled that they did. Koya didn't know what they had done wrong, and Ms. Harris didn't tell them.

"Well, *act* like it," Ms. Harris said. She blew the whistle for them to start, and almost as soon as they did, she blew it again.

"Just *move* out of the way," she said, waving them aside. She beckoned to the other group. "Come on, *show* them how to do it."

She walked a few steps away, shaking her head in disgust. She wore a leotard and tights, and her body was not plump enough for her face, as if they might not belong together.

The new turners took their places, and Loritha and Dawn jumped in. Their faces were unhappy, and Koya could tell that they weren't doing their best. They weren't making mistakes, and Dawn was as graceful as ever, but they jumped as if their brains were floating the messages to their bodies, instead of zinging them.

Ms. Harris stopped them in the middle of the routine and turned on Dawn. "No *wonder* nobody can do anything right," she said. "If the team *captain* can't set a good example, why do I expect anybody *else* to do a good job?"

Dawn's lips formed a pout, making dimples

appear in her cheeks. She lifted her hands to explain. "Ms. Harris — " she started.

Ms. Harris interrupted her. "Everybody just *change* your clothes and go on home," she said. She walked toward her office, leaving the girls standing in the middle of the floor.

Later, walking home, Koya listened as Dawn and Loritha complained about Ms. Harris.

"She makes me sick!" Dawn said.

"Me, too," Loritha said. She jerked her book bag up onto her shoulder. "Getting on us about nothing. One day she hates everything we do and the next day, she's all in the rope, jumping and having fun."

It always fascinated Koya to watch Loritha's expressions traveling across a face that was so much like their father's. High forehead, high cheekbones, squarish chin. Everything except the mustache, only softer.

They reached the row of shops a block from the school, and Dawn and Loritha were fussing so much, they forgot to wave at Mr. Dawson, cutting hair in the window of the barbershop. Koya wished they would change the subject. It was a perfect April day. Warm, but not too warm. Breezy, but not too breezy. It was not a day for anger. The streets were filled with people on their way to or from somewhere, and it seemed to Koya that everybody was enjoying the day, except them.

"Maybe she's tired some days," Koya said, making an excuse for Ms. Harris.

"Maybe she's mean!" Dawn said.

"But — " Koya started, but Loritha didn't give her a chance to finish.

"There you go, Koya," she said, "making excuses for everybody, even when they're wrong."

Koya put her fist up to her mouth as if it were a microphone, stretched her other arm out to the side, and began to sing in a warbly voice.

"There she go-oes, Miss A-mer-i-caaa."

Dawn and Loritha laughed and joined in with her, singing the next line of the song. Then they took turns warbling other old songs. Koya was happy. She had made them laugh. They turned up Dawn's street, a long, tree-lined block of rowhouses, and walked up the hill, still singing, until they reached her house.

After they said good-bye, Koya and Loritha continued the block-and-a-half walk home. Their street, Ferguson, was not so long. The two-story brick houses were semidetached and set back from the street.

"Ma, we're home!" Koya called as they entered the house.

"I'm in here," her mother called back.

Her voice came from the study, just to the right of the entrance hall. Koya and Loritha went in.

"Hi, Ma," Koya said.

Ms. DeLaney didn't look up from the computer right away. She finished the line she was typing, then took a pen and made a mark on the page she was typing from, so she'd know where she had left off. Then she looked up. Her face under her short Afro had soft angles, and her eyes were wide and deep-set, like Koya's. She smiled, and it was the special smile she saved just for her daughters.

"Hey, girls," she said. Her voice was slightly low and had the kind of catch in it that Gladys Knight had when she sang.

Loritha kissed her mother's cheek and sat down on the large couch against the wall.

Ms. DeLaney opened her mouth to talk, but Koya beat her to it, asking the questions she knew her mother was going to ask, and answering them, too. She leaned left and right, turning her head back and forth as if she were two people having a conversation.

"Everything go okay at school?" "Yes, Ma." "You had a good day, huh?" "Yes, Ma." "Anything special happen?" "No, Ma. Now, can I get my snack, Ma?"

Ms. DeLaney had laughed through the whole act, and Koya loved it. Her mother was her best audience.

"Sure," Ms. DeLaney said, "but I have some good news you might want to hear first."

"What? What is it?" Koya asked. She sat down beside Loritha.

"Wait, not so fast," Ms. DeLaney said. "What about your day, Ritha?"

"It was okay," Loritha said. Her answer was short, so Koya could tell she was eager to hear the good news, too. Loritha always sounded calm, even when she wasn't.

"Ma!" Koya said. "What's the news?"

"There's a letter over on the table," her mother said.

Koya walked over to the long table in the corner where her mother kept her work. The envelopes were stacked neatly, large gray ones, large and small brown ones, white ones of all sizes, all containing work that her mother would type for other people.

"Which one?" Koya asked.

"You mean you don't see it?" her mother said, laughing.

Then Koya spotted the letter with the New York postmark and the familiar handwriting. It was from her cousin. "It's from Delbert, Jr.!" she said. "What did he say?"

"Read it," her mother said.

But Koya was too excited to take it out of the envelope. "What did he say?" she repeated, jiggling the letter up and down.

Loritha's excitement was only in her eyes. "Is he coming for a visit?" she asked.

Her mother nodded.

"When?" Koya asked.

"In two weeks," her mother said.

Koya screamed and hugged the letter.

Her mother and Loritha laughed at her, and she wasn't even trying to be funny.

Two

That evening, after Koya's father had come home from work at the drugstore, and they had all eaten dinner and cleaned the kitchen, everybody except Koya was doing what they usually did.

Her mother was back at her desk, this time studying for the accounting class she was taking. Loritha had finished her homework and was curled up in the large swivel chair in the living room, reading a mystery. And Mr. DeLaney, sitting on the couch across the room from Loritha, was reading a magazine for pharmacists and making notes on blue index cards. From time to time, he stopped to think, and his face had the happy serious look it always had when he read about medicines.

Usually, Koya would have been lying on the living room carpet, doing homework. But not today. Today, she was lying on the carpet reading Delbert's letter, again, and her books, beside her on the floor, had not been opened.

Delbert's letter began *Dear Everybody*, and Koya knew it was going to be one of his funny letters. But she had been wrong. Delbert was in a serious mood.

Dear Everybody,

As you know, some wonderful things have happened to me in the past few months. A hit record! Can you believe it? Sometimes I almost can't believe it myself — that after so much pain and disappointment, my music is finally reaching a lot of people. They write me beautiful letters, telling me how much the music means to them.

None of this would have happened if it hadn't been for you. I've been trying to think of a way to thank you, and I knew you wouldn't accept anything for yourselves. So I've arranged to come down there, with Sherita and the band, and do a benefit show for the homeless shelter, the one on Paige Avenue. You'll be the only ones who'll know that it's really in your honor. The show is at the Mills Theater on the 30th of this month.

I'm really looking forward to seeing you. I hope we can spend some quiet time together.

Love,
Delbert

Koya read the last line again, then she sat up. "Listen to this part, Daddy," she said.

"You've already read the whole letter to me twice, Koya," her father said. He looked up from his notes, but his mind didn't follow right away.

"But listen," Koya said, "listen, Daddy."

Her father's eyes focused on her, and she continued.

"Do you think this means he's going to stay with us instead of at a hotel or something?" She read the words slowly, with emphasis on each one. "He says, 'I hope we can spend some quiet time together.' What do you think?"

"I think it means he hopes we can spend some quiet time together," Mr. DeLaney said, laughing.

"Daddeee," Koya said, dragging out the word, "I'm serious. What do you really think?"

"Well, I don't know, Koya," her father said. "We can try to talk him into staying here. But, you know, he may need to stay where the band stays."

That wasn't what Koya wanted to hear. She turned to Loritha. "Ritha," she said, "what do you think?"

"Huh?"

Loritha didn't raise her eyes from the book, and Koya knew her sister was in another world. It would be useless to try to talk to her now. She folded the letter, laid it on the coffee table, and started on her history homework.

An hour later, she had finished. Her father was reading the newspaper now, and Loritha had gone up to her room to watch television. Koya got up off the floor and sat in the swivel chair. She swung it slowly back and forth, daydreaming about the whole family sitting up late, talking to Delbert.

In a little while, her mother came into the room, stretching and sighing.

"Rough, huh?" Mr. DeLaney said.

"Rough isn't the word!" his wife answered.

She sat on the couch beside him, and he put his arm around her and gave her a quick kiss on the back of her neck.

Ms. DeLaney pointed to the magazine on the coffee table. "Anything good?" she asked her husband.

"Yeah, some great stuff," he said, "on herbal medicines."

Koya watched her mother and father look at each other and laugh about nothing, and she knew they were thinking about the day when they could afford to open their own pharmacy. Her mother would be the accountant.

Ms. DeLaney slipped off her loafers and tucked her legs under her. "Where's Ritha?" she asked.

"I'll get her," Koya said. She went to the bottom of the steps. "Ritha," she called, "Ma's finished her homework."

Koya went to the kitchen to get juice for everybody. She got their favorites, pineapple for her mother, orange for her father and Loritha, and grape for herself. She set the glasses on a tray and took it to the living room. Loritha had come down and was seated on the floor, her back against the big chair, and Koya sat down beside her.

"What do you all want to do?" Koya asked. "Want to go downstairs and play some Ping-Pong?"

Her father looked at her mother. "Yvonne, you're not up to that, are you?" he asked.

Ms. DeLaney answered by letting her shoulders slump and her arms flop, as if she were about to fall over, and everybody laughed.

"What about charades?" Loritha asked.

"Okay," her mother said. "But why don't you go first, Maurice? Koya and Ritha will do something hard, like some rock star I've never even heard of."

Mr. DeLaney got up and stood in the middle of the floor. He thought for a moment, then he said, "Okay, this ought to be pretty easy. The category is movies." He put his thumb and his forefinger close together to give the clue for a short word.

"Is it *the*?" Ms. DeLaney asked. "Is the first word *the*?"

Mr. DeLaney nodded.

"*The Cosby Show*!" Koya shouted.

Her mother, father, and Loritha stared at her.

"He said *movies*!" Loritha said. "You're not paying attention, Koya."

"Wait," her father said. "Forget about charades. I know the perfect game for tonight. It's a great new game called Talking About Delbert."

"Sounds like a bet to me!" Koya said, laughing.

"Okay, I'll start," Mr. DeLaney said, "since I knew him first."

He talked about being almost a teenager when his big brother, Delbert, got married and had a son and named him Delbert, Jr.

"I was so proud about being an uncle," Mr. DeLaney said, "I played that role to the hilt!

And when he was three or four, and started picking out tunes on the piano, my chest was stuck out more than his mama's and daddy's."

Everybody had a Delbert, Jr., story to tell. They took turns talking about the happy memories, and Koya was glad nobody mentioned the really sad one. They talked until ten o'clock, Koya and Loritha's bedtime. It was Koya's turn to brush her teeth first. She started up the steps, but her mother's voice stopped her before she got very far. She turned around to listen.

"You know, girls, I was just thinking," her mother said. "It might not be a bad idea to keep our news a little quiet. Otherwise, I'm afraid we won't have much time alone with Delbert. Have you told many of your friends that you're related to him?"

"Oh, no, we already thought about that," Loritha said. "That if Delbert, Jr., came to visit, everybody would be hanging around and everything, trying to meet him. So we kept it a secret. We only told Dawn."

Koya felt suddenly hot, but she tried not to change her expression. "Okay, good night," she said. She continued up the steps and went into the bathroom. She closed the door and leaned against it.

"Right," she whispered, "just Dawn. And Angie, and Contee, and Michael, and Ms. Thomason, and . . ."

She counted the names on the fingers of both hands, and when she ran out of fingers, she knew she was in big trouble. Loritha was going to be mad.

Three

The next morning, Koya couldn't wait to get away from Loritha. In her unexcited way, Loritha was as excited about Delbert's visit as she was, and Loritha wasn't going to like it one bit that she had told the secret.

"I'm so glad we didn't tell anybody," Loritha said to Koya, on their way to pick up Dawn for school.

"Me, too," Koya said. She wanted to laugh, partly because she felt silly watching herself act, and partly because she was nervous.

"Especially that Contee," Loritha said. "He can't keep anything to himself. I'm glad we didn't tell him."

"Yeah, me, too," Koya said.

"I felt like telling *ev*-er-rybody," Loritha said.

"Me, too!"

Koya was having a hard time keeping herself

from giggling. She had never "me too-ed" so much in her life. She hoped she could make it to school without giving herself away. She tried to speed up, but Loritha kept walking in her same slow way.

When they reached Dawn's house, she was waiting for them on the porch. She came quickly down the steps, each movement of her arms and legs flowing smoothly into the next.

"Our cousin's coming week after next," Loritha told her. "They're coming to do a show."

"Coming here?" Dawn said. "Del and Sherita are coming *here*?"

"Shhh!" Loritha said, looking around at the groups of children walking nearby.

Dawn lowered her voice. "Nobody big ever comes here. They really coming, no kidding? We don't have to go to Philadelphia, or D. C.?"

"No kidding," Koya said, absentmindedly. She was thinking about something else.

She didn't know why she had told so many people about Delbert. She had always been good at keeping secrets. But somehow, back in December, when all the radio stations were playing "Makin' a Home" over and over, and her classmates were singing it, and talking about it, and dancing to it, her mouth just kept popping open without her permission.

Twelve different times, to twelve different people, she had blurted out, "Don't tell anybody, but Del is my cousin!" The looks on their faces, once they realized she wasn't joking, were almost worth the trouble she was going to get into with Loritha.

Almost, but not quite.

"Don't tell *anybody*," she heard Loritha whisper to Dawn, just as they reached the school door, " 'cause they'll want to know how you found out." And Koya suddenly wondered what were the chances of a dozen people in one classroom losing their memory all at the same time. She didn't think she'd better count on it. She just hoped her friends could keep *their* mouths shut better than she had.

Before she had a chance to put her books on her desk, Lisa, the girl in the class who always wanted attention, came running in.

"Guess what, everybody!" she said.

Most of her classmates didn't bother to look up, but Koya noticed the reddish tinge of excitement under the brown of her skin.

"No, really, y'all," Lisa said. "Guess who's coming to the Mills Theater!"

Koya's heart bumped against her chest. Everybody stopped what they were doing and turned to Lisa. She waited, keeping them in suspense. The front of her long, black hair had been combed loosely across her forehead so that every time she bobbed her head, the hair fell over her eyes, and she had to shake it back.

"Who?" a boy finally asked.

"They're coming soon!" Lisa said.

"Who?" another boy asked.

Lisa dragged it out further, enjoying the spotlight. She shook her hair. "I saw the poster on a fence near my house."

"*Who??*" A chorus of impatient voices.

"Del and Sherita!" Lisa said.

Twelve heads snapped toward Koya, then jerked away. The rest of the class was asking Lisa, "When?" and Koya joined in. "*When? When?*" she said, louder than anybody.

All through the day, whenever they had a free minute, or when Ms. Thomason left the room, the children talked about the show, about how they were going to beg their parents to take them to see it, even if they had to give up Christmas and birthday presents, or wash pots and pans at the burger shop for the rest of their lives to pay their parents back.

One by one, Koya's friends came up to her, whispering.

"Aren't you excited?" they asked.

"Yeah," Koya told them. "But don't tell anybody." And they all promised they wouldn't.

At lunchtime, on the playground, Devann, a boy who didn't know the secret, came over to Koya. "Why is everybody whispering?" he whispered.

"They have laryngitis?" Koya said.

"Naw, come on," Devann said.

"Okay," Koya said. "They don't want to disturb the class."

"Hey, you can tell me," Devann said. "I won't tell nobody."

"You sure?" Koya asked.

Devann nodded, and Koya looked around for eavesdroppers. Then she leaned toward Devann's ear and said, "We're going to boycott school one day next week."

"Why?"

"Too much homework."

"All *right*!" Devann said. "Just let me know the day!" He walked away, beaming.

When the last bell of the day rang, Koya felt good. Everything was perfect. Devann was off her case, thinking about a boycott that would never take place, and all the people who knew the secret were getting stiff necks from trying not to look at her whenever somebody mentioned the show.

Now, Loritha wouldn't be mad at her, and this crazy, crazy day was over. She laughed to herself as she headed toward the gym to watch double-dutch practice.

Four

The next morning, her happy bubble was burst by a stranger.

"Hey! Are you all really Del's cousins?"

Koya felt as if she had been suddenly bopped on the back of the head. A ripple ran through her stomach. She and Loritha were on their way to school, hardly half a block from home, when the girl ran up behind them, breathing hard, as if she had been running for her life.

"Uh-huh," Loritha answered, and the girl fell in step beside them as if they had been walking to school together all their lives.

Loritha looked at Koya. She was angry. "Dawn blabbed!" she said.

Koya felt the ripple again. "I don't think it was Dawn," she said softly. The ripple moved up through her chest and throat, turned into a tiny nervous giggle, and escaped into the air. Loritha recognized the sound.

"*You* blabbed!" she said. "Why'd you do that, Koya?"

"I couldn't help it, Ritha," Koya said.

"Yes, you could!" Loritha said.

The strange girl was walking happily between them, looking back and forth into their faces as they talked, and Koya wondered how she kept from tripping, since she wasn't looking where she was going.

Dawn joined them, and now there were four of them squeezed together on the sidewalk. Other children passing by were staring at them and pointing at them, and children they usually smiled at and said "hi" to were waving at them as if they were long lost friends. Everybody knew.

Koya leaned around the girl and looked at Loritha's face. It didn't look happy. Koya felt Loritha's anger as if it were a monster glaring down at her, shrinking her and shrinking her, and just before she shrank into nothing, she did the only thing she could do to try to save her life. She made a little joke.

"We're as famous as Patti LaBelle, and we can't sing a lick."

Loritha didn't crack a smile, but Koya tried again. "We're as famous as Michael Jordan, and we can't dunk a doughnut. We're as famous as — "

"Okay!" Loritha snapped. "I'm not mad!"

It hit all of them at the same time, the difference between what Loritha had said and the way she had said it. Loritha started to laugh first, and then they all laughed, Koya the hardest of all, because her sister wasn't mad anymore.

They were still laughing — Koya, Dawn, Loritha, and the stranger — as they walked into school together like a big, happy family.

Five

Koya couldn't get to her classroom. She was surrounded in the hall by children who wanted to talk to her and touch her. She could hear, "Del's cousin, she's Del's cousin," echoing through the corridor. She could still feel the stranger, stuck to her like Krazy Glue, but she had lost sight of Dawn, and the last she saw of Loritha, she was being swept toward her room by another group of children.

Koya felt like a star. She was beginning to like this new fame, and she liked it even more when she saw that one of her fans was Winston, the boy she liked from the other sixth-grade class. His friend, the one Dawn liked, was with him. Fine and Fine Two. That's what she and Dawn called them behind their backs.

She didn't want Winston to know she liked him, so she looked away quickly, and when she sneaked a look back, Dr. Hanley, the principal, was standing there, dressed, as usual, in a suit and colorful head wrap, and holding her reading glasses in her hand. She didn't say a word. She just looked around at the crowd, with a small frown on her face, as if she were puzzled that such a thing could happen in her school. It was a look the children knew well, and as soon as they saw it, they quieted down and the groups broke up.

When Koya finally got to her room, minus the stranger who had disappeared, almost everybody wanted to talk to her. Koya tried to catch Dawn's eye, to see if she had seen the two Fines, but Dawn didn't look her way.

Ms. Thomason was standing at her desk. "Boys and girls," she said, "boys and girls, settle down now."

A boy named Rodney raised his hand. He was wearing his brother's too big, football letter sweater, and his hair was cut as close as it could be without shaving.

"But, Ms. Thomason — " he said.

Angie interrupted. "Can't we talk to Koya for a minute?" she said in her tiny girl voice.

"Maybe later," Ms. Thomason said. "Get your notebooks out now."

While the class was still getting settled, she called Koya to her desk.

"I hope all this commotion isn't getting on your nerves, Koya," she said.

"It's okay," Koya said, as if she were bored with all the celebrity stuff. But she was thinking something else. *I love it! More! More!*

"I was wondering," Ms. Thomason continued, "if you would mind answering some of the students' questions about your cousin. Just for a few minutes?"

Koya shrugged. "No, I don't mind," she said. She hoped she sounded as if she could take it or leave it.

After Dr. Hanley made the morning announcements on the intercom, Ms. Thomason told the class what she had planned.

"But only if you agree to work extra hard the rest of the day," she said.

"We will!" Contee said it first, so excited he forgot to squint, and the other voices followed.

Koya went to the front of the room, so she could call on the students as they raised their hands. Almost every hand shot up immediately, but Koya called on Rodney first. She knew his question would be long and filled with big words, and she wanted to get it over with.

"I've read," Rodney said, taking his time,

"that fame is a mixed blessing and not as much to be desired as we have been led to believe. Has your cousin expressed his philosophy about that?"

"No," Koya said, "not yet."

Michael's hand was up. He almost never raised his hand, and Koya was surprised until she realized that he wanted to stand up and show off his new, blue jacket. She called on him.

"How much money does Del make?" he asked.

Koya didn't know. "Kind of a lot, I think," she said.

"What kind of car does he drive?" a girl asked.

Koya didn't know. "Kind of a medium-sized, big car," she said.

"Does he have a lot of girlfriends?"

She knew the answer to that one. "He only has one girlfriend. She goes to college, and she's real nice."

"Does he know Stevie Wonder?"

Koya didn't have the slightest idea. "I guess so," she said. "He knows a lot of musicians."

She was disappointed. They wanted to talk about what he had and who he knew. She wanted to talk about *him*, about how much he loved music, and how he could almost make his horns talk, and how easy it was to tell him things.

She was glad when it was over and she could go back to her seat. She didn't think they even cared about Delbert. They just wanted to talk about any famous person. She felt let down.

When it was time for lunch, the class lined up in twos and walked quietly through the halls. Dr. Hanley didn't care about straight lines or silence, but she did care about good manners. The students chatted softly as they walked.

Ms. Thomason went with them as far as the door of the multipurpose room, which was sometimes the auditorium and sometimes the lunchroom. She reminded them to behave, then took Rodney aside.

"No karate!" she said. She gave him a stern look before she left.

In the mixture of smells, Koya thought she detected spaghetti sauce, and when she got to the steam table, she was happy to discover that she had been right. She got her food and took her tray back to the table where she and Angie and Dawn and Contee and Michael always sat.

She was hoping nobody would mention Delbert, and nobody did. Things were just about back to normal. Only a few children stared at her as they passed by, and although the strange girl — she said her name was Carinne — sat with them for a little while, she soon became bored with the regular conversation and left.

Koya was glad to see her go. She wanted to laugh and talk with her friends. Then she noticed that Dawn wasn't saying much. Michael was the one who was always kind of quiet, but today, Dawn was quieter than Michael. And Koya thought she knew why. Dawn was feeling left out from all the attention on Koya.

"When's the double-dutch competition?" Koya asked, trying to make her talk.

"You know when it is," Dawn said.

"I forgot."

"How could you forget? It's next week," Dawn said.

"You all are going to win," Angie said.

"Well, we still got a lot of practicing to do," Dawn said.

"I got a good idea," Contee said. "Let's all go to the last practice. We can do some cheers when they finish."

"I could make up one," Michael said.

"Don't even try it," Contee said, and everybody laughed. Dawn, too. They all knew Michael couldn't keep time.

"What about this?" Koya said. "Barnett, Barnett, that's our school, we got a team that ain't no fool . . . uh, uh . . ."

Contee shook his fist in a steady rhythm. "Don't try to win at double-dutch," he said, " 'cause Barnett's team is just too much!"

"Yaaaay, team!" Angie said, throwing her arms up. The loudness of her voice startled her friends. The teacher on duty turned to glare at her, and Angie snatched her arms down.

At the end of the day, Koya didn't go to the gym. It was Friday, so she and Angie went to the auditorium, where the Drama Club met each week with Mr. Fillmore. They stood in a little group near the stage, watching the door at the back of the auditorium, waiting for Mr. Fillmore to make his grand entrance.

"Here he comes!" one of the boys said.

Today, Mr. Fillmore didn't have on a false mustache or a wig, or any kind of costume, except a wide-brimmed black hat cocked to one side. Koya watched him closely as he walked slowly down the aisle toward the stage. It wasn't really the hat that changed him. It was his posture. He was still slim, almost skinny, and tall, but his shoulders weren't *quite* as straight as usual. His knees were *slightly* bent. His feet pointed a *little* outward. He didn't swing his arms. And he was no longer Mr. Fillmore.

The children applauded, as they did almost every Friday when he came in. It was only once in a while that they told him, "Naw, Mr. Fillmore, you still look like yourself."

Mr. Fillmore took off the black hat and laid it on the stage, and the children gathered around him.

"Okay, what was different?" he asked.

They told him about his arms and knees and shoulders and feet.

"What else?" Mr. Fillmore asked.

"The hat," Gerard Brown said.

"What else?" he asked.

They tried to remember.

"It was your face," Koya said.

"What about my face?"

"I don't know," Koya said. "Just . . . something."

"Like this?" Mr. Fillmore asked. He sucked in his cheeks, just a little, and tightened some of the muscles in his face. "You try it," he said, "and see if you can feel the difference."

He let them make faces for a few minutes and told them to try it again in front of a mirror when they got home. Then he passed out a script for a short play he wanted them to present before school closed. There were enough parts for all of them, and they helped him decide who would play which parts.

Two people wanted to be the main character, a girl who was always arguing, and they had to vote. But for the character who was silly, everybody wanted Koya, and the part of the little kid went to Angie.

On her way home, Koya was glad that the double-dutch team was practicing every day now, getting ready for the competition. That meant she could walk home alone today. She could change her face and her walk the way Mr. Fillmore had changed his, without Dawn and Loritha teasing her. Sometimes they'd walk behind her and giggle, or pretend they didn't know her. They said people would think they were *all* crazy, not just Koya.

But Koya liked to watch people to see what they would do when they saw her. It was fun. That was the way *she* practiced. The people walking down the street were her audience.

She walked the four blocks home with her arms at her sides, not swinging, her cheeks sucked in, and her shoulders down. She thought she looked like a very unhappy child. But three people smiled at her, as if she were playing a game. She guessed she hadn't done it right.

She'd try again later, in front of her mirror.

Six

Loritha had beaten her home. She was already in the kitchen, slicing cucumbers while her mother mixed chicken salad. That meant Koya and her father would have the job of cleaning the kitchen after dinner. Koya could never make up her mind which job she would rather do. When she was cooking, she wanted to be the one who would clean up, and when she was cleaning up, she always wished she had helped with the cooking.

Her mother looked up with a teasing smile, and Koya knew Loritha had told her what had happened at school that morning.

"Couldn't keep the secret, huh?" her mother asked.

"I don't usually tell things," Koya said, glancing at Loritha. She didn't want Loritha to think she would ever tell any of their real secrets.

"I know you don't," her mother said. Loritha grinned at Koya, reminding her silently of some of the secrets they shared, and Koya knew everything was all right. "Anyway, I hear you two had a big day."

"Too big," Koya said.

"Yeah," Loritha said. "It was fun for a while, though. A boy in my room even asked me for my autograph."

"Did you give it to him?" Koya asked.

"No," Loritha said, laughing at the thought of it.

"Why didn't you?" Koya asked. "You could've signed it *Del DeLaney's Gorgeous Cousin*, or something like that."

"Ma," Loritha said, "do you think Delbert, Jr., would visit our school?" She dumped the cucumbers into a bowl with other vegetables and began to toss the salad.

"I don't know about that, Ritha," Ms. DeLaney said. "He's going to be so busy."

"Well, we could ask him," Koya said. "Couldn't we call and ask him?"

"I don't think you should . . ." Ms. DeLaney began.

"He won't mind," Koya said. "He can say no if he wants to. We'll tell him he can say no if he wants to."

"You know he'll break his neck trying to do whatever you ask him to do," Ms. DeLaney said. "But go ahead, I guess it's all right. And don't start begging and acting pitiful if he can't do it."

"Can we call right now?" Loritha asked.

Ms. DeLaney glanced at the wall clock. "Wait fifteen minutes," she said, "till the rates go down. We need that money more than the phone company does. It can go right into — "

" — the four-year pot. I know," Koya said.

Two years ago, they had called it the six-year pot, last year it was the five-year pot, and now it would be just four years before her mother and father had enough money to open their own pharmacy.

At one second past five, Loritha was dialing the living room phone, with Koya standing almost as close to the receiver as she was. After the fourth ring, there was a click followed by soft music.

"Hey." It was Delbert's voice on the answering machine. "Leave a message. Short and sweet. You got thirty seconds."

"Delbert, Jr., this is Ritha," Loritha said, as calm and slow as usual. "We want to know if you can — "

"Hurry up!" Koya said. "You're talking too slow!" She leaned into the receiver. "Call us!

Can you visit our school? What day are you coming? You're going to stay at our house, aren't you?" She got it all in before time was up.

Mr. DeLaney sipped the last of his tea. "Great dinner," he said, glancing at his wife and Loritha. He dabbed his mouth with the paper napkin. "So, where're we going tonight?" he asked.

"I don't want to go out," Loritha said. She ate the last forkful of her mixed vegetables.

"Neither do I," Koya said.

Mr. DeLaney looked surprised. "What do you mean you don't want to go out? It's Friday night."

"They're waiting for Delbert, Jr., to call," Ms. DeLaney explained. "There's no way we're going to get them to leave the phone."

"Well, how about switching nights," Mr. DeLaney said. "Make tomorrow family night out, and you and I go out tonight."

"Want to take in a movie?" Ms. DeLaney asked.

"Sounds good to me. And tomorrow, why don't we visit the Tuckers? We haven't been over there for a while."

"No, let's go bowling," Loritha said.

"I had hoped we could go to that jazz concert up at the university," Ms. DeLaney said. "It's only going to be there one night."

"What about you, Koya?" her father asked.

"I don't care," Koya said. "Whatever you all want to do."

"You always say that," Loritha said. She was irritated.

"Okay, let's vote," Ms. DeLaney said.

Koya hated to hear those words. She knew everybody would vote for their own choice, and her vote would have to be the deciding one. She really wanted to go bowling, but she didn't want to take sides with anybody. She stood up and began stacking the dishes.

"I vote for bowling," Loritha said.

"Concert," Ms. DeLaney said.

"The Tuckers," Mr. DeLaney said.

Then everybody turned to Koya.

"Coin time!" Koya said, laughing.

"*Koya!*" They all spoke at the same time.

"Come on, now, Koya," her father said. "We're not deciding who's going to be hanged at dawn, just where we're going tomorrow night."

"Get a coin, Daddy," Koya said.

" 'Get a coin, Daddy,' " Loritha said, imitating her.

Mr. DeLaney stood up and took a penny from his pocket. "Okay," he said, "heads we go to the concert, tails we go bowling."

He flipped the coin. It came up tails.

"Okay, that eliminates the concert," Mr. DeLaney said. "Now, heads it's the Tuckers, tails it's bowling."

He flipped again, and this time it came up heads.

"Yuk!" Loritha said.

Koya felt the same way. Mr. and Ms. Tucker were nice, but it was the house that made her sick. Almost every room was decorated in a greenish yellow — carpets, curtains, bedspreads, almost everything. Koya called it "barf yella." And every room, even the bathroom, had a speaker that carried music from the living room radio. It was the *nothing* kind of music they always played on elevators.

Koya scraped the garbage from the plates while her father ran water in the sink. He washed and she dried.

"So, what did you really want to do?" her father asked, after her mother and Loritha had left the room.

"Go bowling," Koya said.

"Why didn't you say so?"

Koya dried a cup and put it in the cabinet before she answered. Then she sighed. "I don't know, Daddy," she said. "I just wanted everybody to be happy."

"Could it be that you were afraid somebody

might be a little angry with you?"

"Well, I don't like for people to be mad," Koya said.

"You can't always please everybody, Koya," her father said, and then he changed the subject. Not like her mother who always wanted to get to the bottom of everything.

Later, after their parents left for the movies, leaving them with a list of emergency numbers and a lot of dos and don'ts, Koya and Loritha watched television and waited for the phone to ring.

Around eleven o'clock, Loritha gave up and went to bed and Koya curled up on the sofa, with the phone beside her. She imagined that the phone cord stretched all the way to New York, and people in Pennsylvania and New Jersey were tripping over it, trying to get wherever they were going. She chuckled to herself. And that was the last thing she remembered until she felt her mother waking her up so she could go to bed.

Seven

Koya woke up early the next morning. Too early for a Saturday. She turned on her stomach and pushed her face deeper into the pillow, but she couldn't go back to sleep. She sat up and looked around the room, trying to decide how she would fix it up for Delbert. If he stayed at their house, she would move in with Loritha.

The phone in her parents' room rang, and Koya jumped out of bed and ran for it, coming out of her room just a step before Loritha came out of hers. When they reached their parents' room, it was empty, and the phone stopped ringing before Koya got to it. She and Loritha waited, trying to hear what was being said on the extension downstairs.

In a moment, her mother called, "Pick up, it's Delbert, Jr."

"Hey, girl," Delbert said, after Koya said hello. "How you doing?"

"I'm fine. How *you* doing?"

"Great."

"What day are you coming?" Koya asked.

"Wednesday after next," Delbert said. "I gave Aunt Yvonne all the details, so you all can meet me at the airport."

"I can't wait," Koya said. "Can you come to our school while you're here?"

"Would Thursday morning be okay? I can squeeze it in, but . . ."

"He can come!" Koya said to Loritha.

". . . but I'll have to come alone," Delbert continued. "Sherita and the band won't be able to get there."

"That's okay," Koya said.

Loritha reached for the phone. "Let me talk," she said.

Koya gave her the phone.

"Delbert, Jr.," Loritha said, "can our principal call you? She says nobody can visit our school, unless she talks to them first and finds out what they're going to say to her children."

Koya had forgotten all about that. Loritha listened, then nodded in Koya's direction. That meant Delbert had said okay.

"Ask him if he's going to stay with us," Koya said.

Loritha asked him and waited for his answer. Then she said, "Okay, 'bye," and hung up.

"What did he say?" Koya asked.

"He said, 'Where else?' "

Koya clapped her hand over her mouth so she wouldn't scream.

"Koya, don't you tell *anybody*," Loritha said.

"Don't worry, I won't!" Koya said. She knew better than to say one word this time.

The rest of the day went too quickly for Koya. With housecleaning, grocery shopping, and homework, it was soon time to go to the Tuckers'.

"Do we have to go?" Loritha asked.

"I think you're going to have a good time," Mr. DeLaney said. "When I called Eddie, he said their niece, Tracee, is visiting from Newark, and she's about your age."

They were starting out the door when Koya stopped suddenly. "Wait a minute," she said, "I forgot something."

"What?" her father asked.

"My barf bag!" Koya said.

Her mother tried not to smile, but Loritha laughed.

"Come on, girl," her mother said, "it's not that bad." She put her arm around Koya and walked her out to the car.

Mr. and Ms. Tucker came to the door together, she smiling and quiet, he already starting a conversation about the next day's basketball game. They were happy to see the

DeLaneys, and Koya was glad to see them, too. Until she stepped into the house and heard the music.

It was a song she loved, Duke Ellington's "Satin Doll." Her parents played it all the time on the stereo at home. But it was supposed to swing. Instead, it sounded the way watery syrup tasted.

Koya wondered how Mr. and Ms. Tucker could always manage to find that kind of music on the radio. She thought there must be a station just for them. She could imagine the radio announcer saying, "This is station T-U-C-K-E-R, your *blah* music station." Behind the Tuckers' backs, she cut her eyes at Loritha and made a face as if she were gagging.

After they were all introduced to Tracee, a tall girl in a ponytail and fluffy bangs, the Tuckers talked with Koya's parents in the living room, while Koya and Loritha played Scrabble with Tracee in the den.

Tracee played as if there were a prize of a trillion dollars waiting for the winner. She argued over every word that was put on the board. She tried to cheat, and she got mad a lot. Usually, Koya was a good Scrabble player, but she wasn't having any fun. She let her mind wander.

Loritha won the first game and Tracee came in second.

"I coulda won," Tracee said, "but I didn't get any good letters." She pointed at Koya and laughed at her for coming in third. "That was pitiful," she said.

Tracee won the next game, and Loritha came in a close second.

"Koya," Tracee said, "why don't you let just me and Loritha play?"

"Why?" Loritha asked.

" 'Cause she don't know how to play, that's why."

"Yes, she does," Loritha said. "She beats me all the time."

"Yeah, I'll bet," Tracee said. "How'd you get so stupid," she asked Koya, "when your sister's so smart?"

Koya laughed. "I take stupid lessons," she said.

"You must have a good teacher," Tracee said.

Koya didn't want to argue. "The best," she said. "He's the author of that famous book, *The Art of Being Stupid.*" She laughed at her own joke, but she was the only one laughing. Loritha's eyes were sending daggers at her, and Tracee looked at her with disgust.

"I quit," Loritha said.

"Me, too!" Tracee said. She swept her hand across the Scrabble board, knocking the letters off and onto the table.

Tracee and Loritha sat down in chairs on

opposite sides of the room. Koya kept her seat at the table and began putting the letters in the box.

"You scared of me, aren't you?" Tracee said. "Aren't you?"

"No, I'm not," Koya said.

"I bet I could come over there and smack you, and you wouldn't even do anything," Tracee said.

Koya put all the letters back, closed the box, and picked up a magazine. She didn't answer Tracee. She was hoping that if she ignored her, Tracee would get bored and stop. And in a little while, she did, and they all sat there, not talking.

Koya pretended to read, patting her foot to the radio, as if there were nothing in the world she loved more than listening to watery music. She felt a familiar uncomfortable squirminess in her stomach. She wasn't afraid of Tracee. She just didn't want to argue. She was glad when her mother came to tell them it was time to go.

"You tired, girls?" Ms. DeLaney asked when they were all in the car. "You're so quiet."

"*I'm* tired," Koya said.

"You should have seen Koya, Ma," Loritha said. "She let Tracee talk to her any old kind of way."

"What happened?" Mr. DeLaney asked. He

drove slowly, relaxed, as if he had really enjoyed the visit.

"Nothing," Koya said. "Tracee's just silly. I didn't even care."

"Koya just sat there cracking stupid jokes," Loritha said.

"Well, that's one way of handling a situation like that," her father said. "Did it work, Koya?"

"No, it didn't," Loritha answered for her.

"I *said* I didn't care," Koya said. "I keep telling you all I don't get angry."

"Everybody gets angry sometimes," her mother said.

"*I* don't," Koya said. She could tell that her mother was going to keep talking.

"Koya . . ."

"Ma, I'm tired," Koya whined.

"All right, Koya," her mother said. "But we're going to talk about this again. I think this not being angry thing is going a little too far. We need to get to the bottom of this."

Koya sighed, closed her eyes, and leaned her head against the back of the seat. She hoped her mother would get busy tomorrow and forget to ask her any more questions. She would be glad when Monday came and she'd be back in school.

Eight

"That's wonderful," Dr. Hanley said on Monday morning, when Koya told her that Delbert had offered to come and spend some time with the students. "But you know I need to talk with him, Koya," she said. She had a careful expression on her face, as if she wanted to be sure she didn't hurt Koya's feelings.

"He said that would be okay," Koya said. She handed the principal the slip of paper on which she had written Delbert's number, and Dr. Hanley said she would call him.

Koya had gotten Ms. Thomason's permission to go to the office as soon as she got to school. She made sure that nobody was close enough to hear when she told Ms. Thomason the reason.

On Tuesday Koya waited for Dr. Hanley to

mention the visit during the morning announcements. But she said nothing about it, and Koya worried that Delbert could have said something that would keep Dr. Hanley from letting him come.

On Wednesday morning, Dr. Hanley stopped Koya and Loritha in the hall when they arrived and asked them to come into her office.

"Can . . . I mean, may, Dawn come, too?" Koya asked.

"Of course," Dr. Hanley said. "Come on in, Dawn."

Dawn hesitated, but Dr. Hanley put her arm around her as they walked into the office. When Dr. Hanley removed her arm, Dawn moved a little away from them and looked in the other direction, as if she were not the least bit interested in anything they might say.

"I talked with your cousin last night," Dr. Hanley said to Koya and Loritha. "He sounds like a wonderful young man, and he has some important things he wants to say to the students. I know your family must be very proud of him."

"We are." Koya and Loritha spoke at the same time.

During the announcements, Koya tried to listen as Dr. Hanley talked about which class had the best attendance, but she was really just holding her breath, waiting for the big announcement.

Her feelings were seesawing. She felt good that Delbert could come to the school, since not all of her schoolmates could afford to go to the show. At the same time, she knew she wasn't ready to be famous again so soon and have people glue themselves to her and ask her all the wrong questions. But on the other hand, she felt so excited about being able to watch Delbert perform on the Barnett stage that she was having trouble keeping her toes still.

"Now, a reminder," the principal was saying. "Don't forget that on this Saturday our very own, wonderful, double-dutch team will be competing for the city championship. Remind your parents that the school board has said we can join the league next year, *if* that's what the community wants. That's a big if, so I hope everyone will come out and show their support. That's at eleven o'clock at Hayden High School."

Finally, Dr. Hanley said, "And now, I have a special announcement. We're going to have a visitor next week. On Thursday morning . . ." She stopped for just a beat, then she said, ". . . the musician *Del* will be here. . . ."

Dr. Hanley said a few more words before she

signed off, but Koya didn't think anybody in the whole school heard her, there was so much cheering. Koya could hear it coming from the rooms on her end of the hall, and in her classroom, the children, all except Dawn, applauded her after Ms. Thomason told them that Koya and Loritha had arranged the visit.

Before they started on their arithmetic, Ms. Thomason helped the class discuss what they might want to give Delbert to thank him for coming. It was decided that Rodney, who was the best artist in the school, would draw a picture of Del while he was on the stage and present it to him as a surprise.

Over the next few days, the school buzzed with excitement. It seemed to Koya that each and every one of her four hundred schoolmates must have asked her whether Delbert was going to stay at her house, and she answered four hundred times that he would be staying at a hotel, and no, she didn't know which one.

The only thing going wrong was Dawn. Whenever anybody mentioned Delbert, Dawn would walk away, or get a faraway look in her eyes, as if she couldn't care less. And then she wouldn't talk to Koya for a long time afterward. Koya couldn't tease her into talking or joke her into laughing. And at double-dutch practice, she wasn't talking to Loritha, either.

At home, Koya and Loritha tried to think of

a way to make Dawn feel important.

"Let's give her a party," Koya suggested, "at the lunch table. Ma can help us make a cake, and we can write her name on it."

"We can put 'Captain' on it," Loritha said. " 'Captain Dawn.' And we can draw a jump rope with the icing."

"Let's have it Monday," Koya said, "because after Saturday, she'll be the captain of the double-dutch champions of the world!"

Loritha laughed. "I hope," she said, crossing her fingers.

On Friday afternoon, a short program was broadcast over the intercom from the principal's office. Dr. Hanley wished the double-dutch team good luck in the competition and presented them with new uniforms. Dawn was there to accept the gift.

"These uniforms are real, real pretty," she said, and Koya could hear the smile in her voice. "And on behalf of the whole double-dutch team," Dawn continued, "I want to thank Dr. Hanley and our teachers, and the students and everybody for giving us this present."

When Dawn came back to the classroom, Ms. Thomason asked her to show her uniform to the class, and everybody crowded around to admire the shiny red jacket with *The Barnett Flyers* written in large black letters across the back, and the black shorts, red socks, and white T-shirt with red lettering. Dawn was glowing and her dimples were deep, but when Koya smiled at her, she turned away.

After school, the team had its final practice, and Koya and her friends were there, ready to do their cheer and the steps they had made up to go with it. But the team had the last-day jitters. They were dropping the ropes, and tripping over the ropes, and stomping at the wrong time. Ms. Harris yelled at them and told them to go on home.

After Loritha had changed her clothes and was ready to go, she and Koya looked for Dawn, but she had already gone.

Koya and Loritha were quiet on the way home, and the walk seemed extra long.

Nine

Koya's father found a parking space a block from the high school, and they all got out of the car and joined the other groups of people of all ages, from babies to grandparents, getting out of cars and buses, in the warm April sunshine, and moving toward the entrance of the school.

Koya loved looking at the double-dutch jumpers, in their many colors, walking throughout the crowd. They were from the six schools that would be competing to be the best in the city.

Inside, the large gym was packed and noisy. Koya had begged Ms. Harris to let her sit with the team, so while her parents headed toward the bleacher seats, she went with Loritha to look for the sign that said BARNETT. They passed the long table filled with trophies, gleaming gold and silver.

Ms. Harris saw them approaching and beckoned to them.

"Loritha," she said when they reached her, "we tried to get in touch with you this morning. Dawn called several times, but your line was busy."

Koya didn't like the way Ms. Harris was talking. Her tone was too gentle, as if she were feeling sorry for Loritha. Koya couldn't imagine why.

"What was she calling me for?" Loritha asked.

"Well, she had thought up a new trick for our freestyle routine," Ms. Harris said. "As a matter of fact, she dreamed it. Isn't that something? She called me early this morning to tell me about it. So we all met at school to practice. It's fantastic. I think it could really put us over."

Loritha looked confused. "You all practiced this morning?" she said.

"I'm sorry we couldn't reach you, Loritha," Ms. Harris said.

Loritha's face looked stunned. "I'm not going to be in the freestyle?"

"I'm so sorry, Loritha," Ms. Harris said, "but you want to win, don't you? Wilson's going to be tough to beat, and this trick could do it for us."

Koya looked over at Dawn, sitting with the team. Dawn was watching them, and Koya could almost see the word *guilty* stamped on her face. She knew Dawn hadn't called.

Loritha was trying to hold back her tears. "But I could learn it now," she said. "We could go to another room . . ." She looked at the clock and knew it was too late.

Ms. Harris was tired of being nice. "There's no *time* for that," she said. "You just have to *accept* this. You two take your *seats*, now."

Loritha asked one of the girls to move down one seat, so she could sit next to Dawn, and Koya took an empty seat two places away.

Loritha's disappointment had changed to anger. "You didn't call me," she said to Dawn.

"I did so," Dawn said. "I can't help it if your line was busy."

"You made that up," Loritha said. "You just didn't want me to be in it. You could have run over to our house, if you'd wanted me to be in it."

"I didn't have time!" Dawn said.

Their voices caught Ms. Harris's attention, and her head snapped around. She walked fast over to Loritha and Dawn and put her face close to theirs. She spoke in a loud whisper.

"*We are a team!*" she said. "I don't want you

to say *another* word about this, or even *think* about it, until this competition is over. Now *concentrate* on what you came here to do, or you're going to embarrass yourselves, your families, the school, and *me*!"

As she walked away, there was a shrill whistle from the far end of the floor. The competition was about to begin.

"Take your seats, everybody." The announcer was Coach Dickinson, the high school basketball coach. He held the microphone in his hand and let the whistle dangle from the chain around his neck. The shape of his stomach could be seen pushing against his bright-green T-shirt. "Take your seats, please."

The people in the audience who had been standing around talking walked quickly toward their seats, holding the hands of their small children to help them up the bleacher steps. When almost everybody was seated, the announcer blew the whistle again, and the room grew quiet.

Koya was sorry now that she had asked to sit with the team. She wanted to be on the other side of the room with the families and her classmates and Dr. Hanley, where she couldn't see that Loritha was hurt and angry and struggling to keep from crying. And where she couldn't see the guilt on Dawn's face.

"Okay, we're ready to start," Coach Dickinson said. "I don't know about you, but I've been really looking forward to this day. Our first citywide competition. Sixth-graders only this year, but if all goes well, next year you won't be able to take two steps without bumping into a bunch of kids jumping double-dutch, everybody from fifth grade through twelfth. Now, I want you to welcome two people who are going to help us make this happen."

He introduced two school board members who stood up to be recognized. Then he introduced the six men and women who were going to judge the competition. Each of the judges went to one of the places on the floor where ropes were laid out. The teams followed. Twenty girls and four boys. Two turners and two jumpers at each place. The turners picked up the ropes. The jumpers stood beside them, ready to jump in. They waited, poised, for the signal that would tell them to begin.

"Take your mark!" the announcer said.

There was a hush in the room.

"Get set!"

Then he blew the whistle, and the jumpers went into the ropes, not jumping fast, but trying to do all the steps they had to do, in rhythm with their partners. Koya kept her eyes on Dawn and Loritha. As she watched, her thoughts flowed in a rhythm of their own.

They move together like twins. Like best

friends. Jump on the right foot, jump on the left, turn around, jump, jump on the right foot, jump on the left. They move together. Like friends.

The judges were watching closely. Everything had to be perfect, or points would be taken off. The ropes couldn't touch. The jumpers had to go in and out of the rope correctly. Their posture had to be right.

The whistle sounded to signal the end of the first event. Ms. Harris was happy, smiling, as the audience applauded and the judges marked their score sheets.

"Freestyle, next!" the announcer said.

One minute of tricks the teams had created themselves. Loritha would have to sit down and let a substitute take her place. She left the floor and walked toward the chairs, smiling a stiff little smile, and Koya knew she was trying not to cry.

She wants to wait. Wait and cry at home. I won't look at her, I won't say anything, or she'll cry, and I'll cry, too.

Loritha took the seat beside Koya, instead of the seat she'd had before, as if she needed to sit close to someone she trusted. Koya leaned closer to her without looking at her.

"Okay, let's go!" Coach Dickinson said. "First team up is Parker!"

The girls from Parker School were nervous.

They dropped the rope twice, and one girl slipped and almost fell, and finished jumping with tears rolling down her face.

Some of the other teams made small mistakes. But Wilson didn't make any. It was the team Barnett would have to beat.

Barnett performed last. Dawn and the girl who was taking Loritha's place jumped into the rope and began circling each other, exchanging places, jumping with knees high. Then they circled in the other direction. Hopped five times on one foot, then on the other. Then the turners began to stomp in rhythm with the jumpers, while still turning the rope. Koya had seen all of these tricks before. Now they were about to begin the new one.

Dawn and the other girl somersaulted out of the rope in opposite directions, jumped up and ran back in as the rope turned faster. Koya caught her breath. No other team had done anything as hard and as beautiful.

The girls somersaulted again, jumped up, and turned to run back in, but the ropes had touched and become entangled.

Koya heard Loritha gasp, and saw Ms. Harris close her eyes and give a small shake of her head. The turners quickly pulled the ropes apart, and the trick was finished, but the mistake had been made. Points would have to be taken off their score.

The last event was speed jumping. Two minutes of jumping as fast as they could. The judges would be counting the number of times the left foot hit the floor. This was Loritha's event. She would be jumping by herself.

The announcer gave the signal, and there was an explosion of movement and sound. Six ropes were whirring. Legs and sneakers flying. People in the audience cheering for their team. "Come on, you can do it! You can do it!"

Loritha jumped, left, right, left, right, left, right, speeding. She leaned forward at the waist, not moving her arms, almost not moving the top part of her body at all, as if her flying legs belonged to another person.

My sister is brave. Nobody knows she's really, really sad. Nobody but me.

"Go, Ritha!" Koya yelled.

The two minutes seemed more like two hours to Koya. She wondered if the whistle would *ever* blow. Loritha's eyes were narrowed, staring at a spot just above the floor. She was breathing through her open mouth, but once, for a moment, she pressed her lips together so tightly that deep lines dented her chin. The lost points had to be made up. Her legs kept churning.

One of the boys on another team was jumping fast, too, but only one person was keeping up with Loritha. The girl from Wilson. It looked like a tie.

The whistle finally blew.

"Yeaaaa, Barnett!" somebody yelled through the applause.

Koya watched in suspense as the judges totaled the scores and gave their decision to Coach Dickinson.

"Wooo! It was a close one!" he said. He wiped his face with an imaginary handkerchief, as if he were the one who had been jumping. It made the audience laugh. "You were great, all of you. Each one of you will receive a certificate, something you can be very proud of. And now, the winners."

He read from the card the judges had given him. "First place, Wilson! Second place, Barnett! Third place, Merritt!" He clapped loudly. "Let's hear it for Wilson! Barnett! Merritt! And all the participants!"

The teams went to the front to receive their trophies and certificates. When it was over, relatives and friends came down out of the stands, and there was hugging and kissing, hand slapping and screaming. Koya ran over to where Loritha was standing with the team and hugged her tightly. Mr. and Ms. DeLaney rushed over, too.

"Girl, you were really something!" Ms. DeLaney said.

Koya looked around and was surprised to see Ms. Harris trying to comfort the girl who had made the ropes tangle. Koya wanted to go over and say something nice, but then she saw Dawn across the room. Dawn saw her at the same time, and came running toward her, laughing, reaching out to hug her.

Koya didn't know what to do. She didn't feel like hugging someone who had been so mean to her sister. But stepping back now, with Dawn's arms so close, would be like slapping the smile off her best friend's face. She couldn't bring herself to do it. She put one arm loosely around Dawn's shoulder.

And that's when she saw Loritha's eyes, looking at her from a few feet away.

Ten

"Who is it?" Loritha asked in answer to Koya's knock.

"It's me, Ritha," Koya said. She had gone to Loritha's room as soon as she'd put her pajamas on. She hoped Loritha would let her in.

"What do you want?" Loritha asked.

Koya opened the door slowly. Loritha was in bed with a book. "I just wanted to explain," she said.

All day she had been thinking about only one thing. Making up with Loritha. While they were having lunch at the restaurant with their mother and father, celebrating Barnett's victory and talking about what Ms. Harris and Dawn had done, and all the rest of the day, making up was all she had really been thinking about.

"Can I come in?" she asked.

Loritha didn't answer, so Koya took that for a yes. She went in and closed the door behind her.

Loritha put her book down, but marked the page with her finger. "Koya, you don't even care about what Dawn did to me," she said.

"I do so care," Koya said. She sat down at the foot of Loritha's bed.

"You could at least be a little mad," Loritha said. "That was really mean, what she did."

"I know it was, Ritha. But she's sorry."

"Did she say she was sorry?" Loritha asked.

"No, but I could tell."

"You're not nobody's mind reader," Loritha said. "And neither am I. And I'm never going to speak to her again, unless she apologizes."

"But, Ritha — "

"You going to still be her friend?" Loritha asked.

"Why can't we all be friends like we were?" Koya asked.

"Because she lied, and she made me miss freestyle, and she's not sorry, that's why," Loritha said. "You make me sick. You always have to be so . . . so *good*. Miss Good Girl. I don't want you in my room!"

"Ritha — "

"Get out of my room!"

Koya sat there for a moment, hoping Loritha

would change her mind. But Loritha picked up her book and didn't look up again, and Koya got up and went across the hall to her own room. She got into bed, but left the light on. Somehow, she felt better that way.

When she woke up the next morning, Koya hoped that Loritha would be speaking to her again, but she soon changed her mind and wished that Loritha wouldn't talk to her at all.

"Good morning, Miss Good Girl," Loritha said when they met in the hall.

And all through the day, Loritha called her Miss Good Girl or, when their parents were around, Miss G.G., which was even worse.

Several times, Koya saw their parents exchange glances, but they didn't say anything. Koya knew what they were thinking. "The girls will work it out." She hoped they were right. She kept watching Loritha for a sign that she might be ready to make friends, but the whole day passed without any change.

On Monday morning, they walked to school together without talking, and when they passed Dawn's house, Koya was glad to see she wasn't waiting outside for them. They entered school and went to their separate classrooms without saying one word to each other the whole morning.

Dawn was already in class, and she was

ready to talk. She held out her wrist to show Koya her new watch.

"Look," she said to Koya, "my mom bought it to congratulate me. Isn't it *bad*?"

"Uh-huh," Koya answered, "it's bad."

"Ms. Harris says she's going to give us a party," Dawn said. She paused, then said, "Is Ritha still mad?"

"My whole family's mad," Koya said. "Ma and Daddy are going to have a talk with Ms. Harris, and Ritha's real mad at you. You have to apologize to her, Dawn."

"For what? I didn't do anything."

"Yes, you did," Koya said. "You didn't call our house like you said."

"I did so!" Dawn said.

Dawn's face was set and hard, and Koya knew she was never going to admit she had been wrong.

"Well, why don't you just say you're sorry, anyway?" Koya said. "And then we can all be friends again."

Dawn didn't answer right away. Then she said, "Well, okay, Koya, if you want me to. But just so we can be friends."

Koya was happy with that. Loritha wouldn't know that the apology wasn't real, and maybe later, after Dawn had had time to think about it, she would really be sorry about what she had done.

* * *

Dr. Hanley was proud of the team. She said so during the announcements. She called the name of each member and congratulated them and Ms. Harris for their fine showing at the competition. She mentioned all the weeks of hard practice they had put in and how it had paid off. Koya knew that was the lesson for the day. Dr. Hanley always had a lesson, but it was never boring because she only said it one time.

"We're going to have a celebration," Dr. Hanley said, "a talent show, here at the school, on Saturday morning, to honor our wonderful team. Mr. Fillmore will be contacting some of you to ask you to perform."

Koya hoped she could be a part of the talent show. Maybe Mr. Fillmore would ask her to recite a poem, and before she recited it, she could say some special words to Loritha and Dawn.

Eleven

Lunchtime that day was almost like old times for Koya, now that Dawn was acting like herself again. All of her good friends together, having fun. Contee even mentioned Delbert, and Dawn didn't get mad.

Koya could see Loritha, over at the other sixth-grade table, talking to her friends. Koya leaned over and whispered to Dawn.

"When you going to talk to Ritha?" she asked.

"After while," Dawn said.

"Why don't you do it now?"

"I'll do it on the way home," Dawn said. "We'll all be together then. Okay?"

Koya liked the idea. They could all make up at the same time. She and Loritha. Dawn and Loritha. It would be a big moment in their friendship, one they would talk about after they grew up. She could almost see it.

Later in the afternoon, Mr. Fillmore sent a boy from his class to ask Ms. Thomason if Koya could come to see him. Koya heard her name and looked up hopefully. Ms. Thomason said yes, and, for two reasons, Koya was glad. It meant that she could get out of geography, and it had to mean that she was going to be in the talent show. She wondered what poem Mr. Fillmore wanted her to do.

She went with the student to Mr. Fillmore's room, where his fourth-graders were working at their desks. It was one of Koya's favorite places. Sometimes the Drama Club met there, and Mr. Fillmore told them all about famous African-American actors. All around the walls were framed photographs of actors in scenes from their plays and movies, some of them from a long time ago. Ivan Dixon and Abbey Lincoln in *Nothing But a Man*, Sidney Poitier and Ruby Dee and Diana Sands in *A Raisin in the Sun*, Ira Aldridge, Canada Lee, Claudia McNeil, Dorothy Dandridge, Paul Robeson.

"Come on in, Koya," Mr. Fillmore said when she entered the room. He stopped writing on the board and came over to her. "I wanted to talk to you about the show."

"You want me to do a poem?" Koya asked.

"Well, I was kind of thinking of something else," Mr. Fillmore said.

Koya didn't know what that something else could be. She couldn't play an instrument, and she knew nobody in their right mind would ask her to sing.

"How'd you like to tell some jokes?"

"Just tell jokes?" Koya asked. "Like Bill Cosby, yeah!"

"Well, sort of like Bill Cosby," Mr. Fillmore said. "But I was thinking more like Koya DeLaney. You have a real talent for making people laugh."

"Okay," Koya said. "I've got some new jokes I made up."

"Great," Mr. Fillmore said. "By the way, I hope you've started writing your jokes down, Koya."

"I don't have to," Koya said. "I won't forget them."

"Why don't you start keeping a notebook?" Mr. Fillmore said. "It might come in handy some day."

He told her that rehearsal for the talent show would be on Wednesday, after school, and he asked her to be ready to tell four or five jokes.

Koya had never thought of writing her jokes down, but she was glad Mr. Fillmore had suggested it. She and Loritha and Dawn could stop at the store on the way home and pick out just the right notebook.

But at the end of the day, Dawn said she had

to hurry home, she couldn't wait the few extra minutes for Loritha. Koya waited in the usual place, in front of the school, but when Loritha came out, she was with another girl, and she acted as if she didn't even see Koya standing there.

So Koya walked home alone, thinking. But she didn't want to hear all of her thoughts. She didn't listen to the voice that said Dawn never had any intention of apologizing. Instead, Koya listened to thoughts of her own misery. She hadn't done anything wrong. She wasn't the one who had told the lie. And she wasn't mad at anybody. She didn't know how she had gotten in the middle of this mess.

She didn't feel like stopping at the store, but she did it, anyway. She bought the first notebook she saw, a red, spiral-backed one, and went on home.

Twelve

"Okay, now, that's enough," Koya's father said. "This thing has been going on for two days, and that's long enough. I want you girls to resolve this, or your mother and I will have to resolve it for you."

Koya had asked Loritha if she'd like to see her notebook, and Loritha had answered, "No, I wouldn't!" And that's when Mr. DeLaney looked up from the book he'd been reading. His voice was firm.

Koya and Loritha looked at each other and then at their father, but neither said anything.

"Your mother spoke on the phone today to Ms. Harris," Mr. DeLaney said. "Did she tell you, Ritha?"

"Yes."

"Okay, so that's straightened out," her father said. "Now, I want you and Koya to get it together, you hear?"

"Yes, Daddy," Loritha said.

Koya said, "Okay, Daddy, we will."

Their father got up and walked toward the kitchen, and Koya knew he was giving them time to talk.

"Dawn said she's going to apologize," Koya said to Loritha.

Loritha looked interested. "She did? When?"

"She said it this morning," Koya said.

"No, I mean when is she going to *do* it?" Loritha asked.

"I . . . I'm not sure," Koya said. She could feel herself looking uncomfortable. "Soon, I think."

"Yeah, right!" Loritha said. "Miss Good Girl!" she whispered just as her mother came down the steps.

Ms. DeLaney stopped right where she was. "Now, listen!" she said. "You two are giving me the blues! We're going to get to the bottom of this, right now. Where's your father?"

Loritha pointed toward the kitchen.

"Maurice," Ms. DeLaney called, "can you come in here for a few minutes?"

She sat on the sofa, and her husband came in and joined her. "Okay," Ms. DeLaney said, "what's going on? Is this about what Dawn did?"

"Yeah, Ma," Loritha said. "Koya doesn't even care."

"Koya?" her father said.

"Daddy, yes I do care," Koya said. "But Ritha wants me to be mad just because she's mad. And I think she's going to stay mad forever."

"I'm not!" Loritha said. "Just until Dawn apologizes."

"What Dawn did was very wrong, Ritha," her father said, "and I certainly think she should apologize. But I also think you're putting too much pressure on your sister."

Ms. DeLaney looked at her husband, and Koya could tell that she disagreed.

"I think Koya *needs* some pressure," Ms. DeLaney said. "She has to learn how to take a stand for what's right."

"Well, yes," Mr. DeLaney said. "But I think we should just talk to her, give her a nudge in the right direction. Not expect her to take this stand right now."

"Yes, but — " Ms. DeLaney stopped talking when she saw the way Koya and Loritha were staring at them. "Maybe we should talk in the kitchen," she said to her husband.

Mr. DeLaney nodded his agreement. "You two sit right there," he said. "We'll be right back."

Koya couldn't believe her parents had been arguing in front of her and Loritha about something like that. Sometimes they argued, but never about her and Loritha. They talked things over when they were alone and then gave them one answer.

Koya had thought this was an easy problem. All Loritha had to do was start acting nice, and things would work themselves out. That's what she thought her parents would say.

She listened to their voices in the kitchen. First there were murmurs, then their voices rose, and then there was a short silence followed by more murmurs. When they returned to the living room, they told Koya and Loritha that they hadn't quite decided how the problem should be handled.

"But we'd like you to call a truce," Mr. DeLaney said, "and treat each other with courtesy until we work this out."

"You know, Delbert, Jr., will be here in a couple of days," Ms. DeLaney said, "and we want him to have a good time. So will you try to act nice for the time being?"

Koya and Loritha nodded, Koya happily and Loritha with her mouth twisted. Their parents each picked up something to read and sat at opposite ends of the sofa. The quiet was heavy, and Koya couldn't stand it. She picked up her notebook.

"I'm going upstairs and write some jokes," she said. "Good night, everybody." She looked at Loritha. "Good night, Ritha."

Her parents said good night, and Loritha

said, "See you," pleasantly. But she glanced at her parents to be sure they had gone back to their reading, and then she gave Koya the look. She didn't have to say the words. Koya knew exactly what she meant.

In her room, Koya sat glumly at her desk. Loritha was giving *her* the blues. Calling her Miss Good Girl, Miss Good Girl, Miss G.G., Miss Good Girl. She *wanted* to be a good person, but not the kind Loritha was talking about. Sweet. Sappy sweet.

Koya put her elbow on the desk and rested her chin in her hand. In her imagination, she saw herself dressed in a frilly bonnet and a frilly pink-and-white dress. Ruffles, she was all ruffles. Her head was leaning a little to the side, and she was smiling. *Look at me, I'm soooo sweet*, the smile said.

The image was so silly, it made Koya laugh a little. She knew she was nothing like that girl. No matter what Loritha said. She opened her notebook to the first page and began to think and write. Later, she heard Loritha come upstairs, and before Koya went to sleep, she heard her parents downstairs laughing.

Thirteen

A Del-and-Sherita fever had taken over the school. It floated like vapor through the hallways, so that no child could escape. On their way to their classrooms, to the lunchroom, to the playground, children could be heard softly singing the words of Del and Sherita's song. "Makin' a home in this world, this world, this funny world, this hurtin' world . . ."

Almost everybody was on their best behavior. Two students had been barred from attending the program for fighting on the playground, and nobody else wanted it to happen to them.

"Just two more days!" Contee said to Koya as they worked together during map study period.

"No kidding," Koya said. "I didn't know that."

"I can't believe it!" Contee said, ignoring her teasing. "Did you see the sign Mr. Fillmore's class made on the computer? It stretches all the way across the hall, and it says, WE LOVE YOU, DEL! in big, big letters. And it's in color and everything. They're going to hang it right where he can see it as soon as he comes in the front door."

Koya couldn't wait for the moment when he would walk through *her* front door. After school, she went straight to her room to try to see how Delbert would fit in it. He would probably have to bring more things this time, she thought, since he was doing the show. More suits, more shoes, more horns. She wanted him to have enough room.

She took all of her clothes out of the closet and laid them on the bed. She took her shoes out of the closet and set them beside the bed. She emptied two of her dresser drawers and put the contents on the bed. Then she stood in the middle of the floor and stared. At the bed. She didn't know what to do with all the stuff. Delbert would have a place to put everything except himself.

She could put some things in Loritha's closet, but what would she do with the rest? Finally, she gave up and just dusted and polished her desk and dresser and the headboard of the bed. She'd figure out what to do before she went to bed.

Later in the evening, Koya's mother called

her and Loritha down to the study. Family meeting, she said, and Koya could tell from her voice what this meeting was going to be about.

"First order of business," her father said, laughing, when they were all seated in the study, "Delbert, Jr.'s only coming for a couple of days, Koya, not a decade. So, I think you can put most of those things I saw on your bed back where they belong."

"Second order of business," Ms. DeLaney said, "serious business. You two know how we feel about family. We're going to have our disagreements, but we can't let these things go on too long. No matter what happens, we love each other, right?"

"Yes," Koya said. She looked at Loritha, but Loritha looked down and didn't answer.

Her mother went on. "Your father and I think that in this case, each of you needs to understand what the other is feeling, and we thought we could help you do that."

"Koya," her father said, "do you know why Ritha is angry with you?"

"She just wants me to be on her side, Daddy," Koya said.

"You mean she wants you to agree with her?" her father asked.

Loritha shook her head. "No, Daddy," she said. "That's not it. I thought Dawn was my friend, and she wasn't, and I just don't see how

Koya can like somebody who was so mean to me."

"Because . . . ?" her father asked.

"Because, I thought . . . I thought Koya loved me." Loritha spoke so softly, Koya had a hard time making out the words.

"I *do*!" Koya said.

"But, Koya, do you see what Ritha's feeling," her mother asked, "even more than anger?"

"Hurt," Koya said, after a moment.

"By whom?" her mother asked.

"By Dawn," Koya said. She waited a long time before she added, "And me." She felt tears in her eyes. "But, Ma," she said, "I can't help it if I'm not the kind of person Ritha wants me to be. She should still know I love her."

Her father said, "How would you have felt if you had seen Dawn slap Ritha?"

Koya felt a wave of heat rush through her. "I would have been — " She stopped herself when she realized what she was about to say.

Loritha was looking at her, surprised.

"You see, Ritha?" Mr. DeLaney said. Loritha nodded.

"But she didn't slap her," Koya said. And as soon as the words were out, she knew what her father had meant. In a way, Dawn *had* slapped Loritha.

Ms. DeLaney took Koya's hand and held it. "You can be angry, Koya," her mother said. "It doesn't mean you're not a nice person. Can you try to understand that?"

"No!" Koya said. "People look ugly when they're mad, and they act ugly, too!"

Her mother chuckled. "Well, it's not always a sweet sight," she said. "But you don't have to act like that if you don't want to, Koya. We just want you to recognize what you're feeling and be able to express your feelings. And to be able to take a stand when it's necessary."

"I already know what I'm feeling!" Koya heard her voice getting away from her. "I don't feel mad! And I don't *want* to feel mad. I just want everybody to be nice!" She started to cry.

Her mother put her arms around her and kissed her forehead. She wiped at Koya's tears with her finger. "It's okay, honey," she said. "Don't cry. We're going to work on it, okay?"

Koya said okay, but she didn't mean it. She didn't mean it at all. She didn't want to be that kind of person, and she wasn't going to let anybody change her, not even her mother and father.

"Can we go now?" she asked.

"Sure," her father said. "Meeting adjourned."

"Koya," Loritha said as they were leaving the study, "want me to help you put your stuff back?"

Fourteen

The next day moved very slowly. Koya waited, and waited, for the time when Delbert's plane would arrive. In class, Ms. Thomason, who was never long-winded, talked forever about the test they were going to take next week, and when she finished, Koya didn't have any idea what she had said.

The best thing about the whole day was that Ms. Harris took the double-dutch team out to a restaurant for lunch, and Koya didn't have to sit across the lunch table from Dawn, fighting with herself, wanting to talk to Dawn and not wanting to talk to her at the same time. The only time she would see Dawn was in class, and Koya wanted to keep it that way.

During lunch Koya tried her talent show jokes out on Angie and Contee and Michael, and had them laughing so much, the bell rang before Contee could finish his food. But at rehearsal that afternoon, she couldn't have *spelled* the word *funny*. Her mind was already at the airport.

When she got home, she helped her mother and Loritha fix Delbert's favorite dinner. Cornish hens with cornbread stuffing, scalloped potatoes, green beans, and pineapple candied yams. They set the dining room table instead of the one in the kitchen, and used the lace tablecloth and the good dishes.

At seven twenty-one, Koya and her family were at the airport, watching Gate 6, waiting for Delbert to come through.

Koya and Loritha saw him at the same time, a young man of medium height and build, looking very much like their father. He was dressed in faded blue jeans and matching jacket.

"There he is," Loritha said.

"There's Delbert, Jr.!" Koya said, pointing. Her mother gently pushed her arm down, but it was too late. A man and a woman waiting at the gate had turned to look.

"Isn't that somebody famous?" Koya heard the man ask.

"He does look familiar," the woman answered. She tapped the shoulder of a young man standing next to her.

"Excuse me," she said. "Is that somebody?" She pointed at Delbert.

The young man looked at Delbert and back at the woman as if she were crazy.

"That's Del!" he said. He rushed toward Delbert, grabbed his hand, shook it hard, and kept shaking it. "Del!" he said loudly. "Your album is bad, man!"

Before Koya could take more than two steps forward, a small crowd had gathered. Almost magically, people had appeared and surrounded Delbert, holding out little pieces of paper that they had snatched from their pockets and pocketbooks for him to sign. He was taking his time talking to each person, and Koya could tell he was enjoying it.

"Might as well wait here till he's finished," Mr. DeLaney said. He was enjoying it, too. And even Koya, as impatient as she had been, was getting a kick out of watching her cousin sign autographs.

The last fan, a teenaged boy, wanted his mother to take a picture of him shaking Delbert's hand, and as soon as they left, Koya ran over and hugged Delbert.

"That was *something*!" she said. "I should've had *my* camera."

"We'd better go," Ms. DeLaney said, "before somebody else recognizes you. I'll get my hug later."

Mr. DeLaney picked up the small black overnight bag, and they walked toward the exit. "Is this all the luggage you brought?" he asked.

"It can't be," Koya said. "He couldn't get forty-two trumpets and fifty saxophones in that little bag."

Delbert laughed and put one arm around Koya's shoulder. "I wish I had that many, Cuz," he said. "No, Sherita's driving the van down tomorrow with the band and the rest of the stuff. I came a day early, so I could spend more time with you all."

He had emphasized the word *van* and looked at Loritha, laughing, when he said it, reminding everybody of the time, a few years back, when they were visiting Delbert and his grandparents, and Loritha had hidden in the van, hoping to go traveling with the group.

Loritha pretended that she hadn't gotten the joke. "What are you looking at *me* for?" she asked.

"The Ritha van caper," Koya said. "Right Delbert, Jr.?" She held out her hand, palm up, and Delbert slapped it twice.

After dinner, the family gathered in the living room to listen to a tape of Delbert's next album. He had brought it to them as a gift.

"It won't be released until summer," he said. He got up and began dancing. "This is the latest thing from us folks up in the big city."

Koya glanced at her mother and was surprised to see that she was smiling. She never let them dance on the carpet. Whenever she caught them doing it, she would point toward the basement, and they knew they had better get down to the rec room, or they'd be sorry.

"Come on," Delbert said to Koya and Loritha, "let me show you how to do it."

Loritha picked up the dance right away, as if she had known it all her life. It took Koya a few minutes to get it, but when she did, she knew she had it because her whole body was working together. It felt right. She reminded herself of the Senegalese dancers she had seen at the theater.

They were all into it, her mother moving her head and neck backward and forward, and her father patting his foot and clapping to the beat, when the doorbell rang. Delbert turned the music down.

"I'll get it," Mr. DeLaney said. He looked through the peephole. "I think it's one of your classmates," he said to Koya as he opened the door.

Loritha looked at Koya.

"I didn't tell *any*body," Koya said. "Honest!" She and Loritha went to the door.

It was Rodney, with another boy, a teenager.

"Is Del here?" Rodney asked.

"You forgot to say good evening," Mr. DeLaney said.

"Oh! Good evening. I'm Rodney, and this is my brother, Kevin." He was rushing his words, not taking a long time the way he usually did. "Is Del here?"

"Well . . ." Mr. DeLaney started.

Del came out from the living room. "It's okay, Uncle Maurice," he said.

Rodney's eyes widened when he saw Delbert, and Kevin changed the way he was standing to cool.

"How you doing?" Delbert said. He shook their hands.

"I like your music, man," Kevin said, but Rodney, who never stopped talking in school, except when he was drawing, was speechless. Koya thought she must be seeing a mirage.

"Sorry we can't ask you to stay, this time, guys," Mr. DeLaney said, "but this is kind of a special family night."

"How did you know he was here?" Koya asked.

"I deduced it," Rodney said, not taking his eyes off Delbert.

"How'd you deduce it, brother?" Delbert asked.

At the word *brother*, Rodney grinned and took a deep breath, suddenly turning back into his talkative self.

"Well," Rodney said, speaking slowly and deliberately, "first, I told myself that since you were coming to visit our school in the morning, in all probability, you would be arriving in town tonight. And then I said that since you were related to the DeLaneys, there would be at least a bare possibility that you would come here. So . . ."

Kevin groaned and tapped Rodney on his almost bald head, but Rodney didn't stop talking.

". . . so, I asked myself what was the worst thing that could happen if I just showed up at the door? Well, Mr. and Ms. DeLaney might just throw me out bodily. But I said to myself, 'Rodney, it's well worth the risk.' So here I am."

"Well, I'm glad you made the right decision," Delbert said. "Listen, can you keep a secret?"

"Yeah!" Rodney said.

"You, too, Kevin?"

"Sure!" Kevin said.

"Okay," Delbert said. "I'm going to give you each a photograph, but you can't tell anybody about it until Saturday, after I've left town."

Kevin said, "Wow!" and Rodney lost his voice again.

Delbert went upstairs and got two copies of a glossy photo from his travel bag, a picture of himself and Sherita onstage, singing, microphones in their hands. He signed them, put them in an envelope, and handed them to Rodney.

Kevin had stopped trying to be cool and looked almost as if he might cry. "Thanks, Del, thanks, man," he said. Then he turned to Koya's mother and father. "And thanks for letting us interrupt the family."

Rodney stopped in the doorway as they were leaving. "This is the most stupendous thing that has ever happened to me in my entire life," he said to Delbert. "I promise not to tell one single soul!"

Twenty minutes later, the doorbell rang.

Fifteen

Through the peephole, Koya recognized the girl on the porch as someone she had seen in the neighborhood. She guessed that the woman with her was her mother.

When Koya opened the door, she saw more people standing on the sidewalk, looking as if they wished they could see right through the bricks of her house.

"I hope you don't mind — " the woman started to say.

But the girl was too excited to wait for her mother to finish. "Rodney called me up," she said. "He said Del was here." She was leaning to the side, trying to see around Koya into the living room.

"Did he tell the whole world?" Koya asked, looking at the growing crowd. Older teenagers, kids Koya's age, and little children escorted by adults were streaming, some running, toward her house.

"No," the girl said. "He just told me, and he

made me promise not to tell anybody. So I only told Pamela and Jerome. Is he here? Can I see him?"

"He's busy," Koya said. Delbert had been telling them about a dream he had about his father.

"Who is it, Koya?" Ms. DeLaney called. She came to the door.

"They want to see Delbert, Jr.," Koya said.

The woman was starting to look embarrassed. "I didn't mean to barge in," she said. "It's just that my daughter . . . we . . ." She was too embarrassed to continue. She took her daughter's hand and started to back up.

"I'm so sorry I can't ask you in," Ms. DeLaney said. "We're right in the middle of a discussion."

But the woman had backed out of the house and turned around before Ms. DeLaney finished her sentence. Still holding her daughter's hand, she walked fast, down the porch steps to the sidewalk, past the crowd, and kept going.

"There's a whole lot of people out there," Koya said when she and her mother went back into the living room.

Del shifted his position on the floor as Koya sat down beside him. "Oh, no," he said. "I was hoping this wouldn't happen. We could have met somewhere else, but I really wanted to come here."

Delbert looked around the room, and Koya knew he was thinking about the summer he had spent with her family, the year his parents died in the fire and all his instruments were burned. He wouldn't listen to music after that. He said he didn't want anything to touch him the way music did. But when he came to visit, Koya's parents had rented a piano and put it in the hall where he had to pass it several times a day. And one day he sat down and played a whole song, and when he finished, he cried for a long time.

"We want Del." The voices were so soft at first that Koya thought she was imagining them. But they grew louder, as if the people outside had been unsure about whether it was the right thing to do, and then decided it was okay. "We want Del! We want Del!" Now they were shouting.

"I'll just go out for a minute and say hello," Delbert said.

Koya followed him to the door and watched from inside.

"Hey, everybody," Delbert said. He stood on the porch, waving. "It's good to see you."

The crowd began to chant. "Del! Del! Del! Del!"

"Your music is *bumpin'*, man," a teenaged boy said.

"And you not too bad yourself!" a young woman called out.

A spiral of laughter wound through the crowd. They were beginning to push forward gradually, from the sidewalk onto the lawn. Koya thought they looked like one huge body with a lot of wriggling parts.

"Thanks for coming," Delbert said. "I hope you'll all come out to the show tomorrow night. It's for a good cause." He waved and started into the house. "Good night."

"How about singing a song?" a man yelled.

The crowd surged forward onto the lawn and the neighbor's lawn, trampling two of the neighbor's rosebushes.

"Watch it! Watch the shrubbery!" Delbert said. "Good night, now."

"Hey, you could at least sing one song," the man said. "You wouldn't be making all that money if it wasn't for us."

Delbert came into the house, and as he was closing the door, Koya heard another man say, "Aw, dude, the man worked for it, you didn't give him nothing."

For a few moments, Koya worried that the man who was angry might throw a rock, or something, through the window. But the sounds drifting in were pleasant. Fading sounds of people talking, some older girls singing, harmonizing, and a child's voice asking, "Did you see him? I saw him. Did you see him?"

When there was no more sound, Delbert went next door to apologize and pay for the damage to the bushes. Koya's father went with him. When they came back, they took a small plastic bag outside and picked up the candy wrappers and other little bits of paper that had been left.

Koya felt limp, weary, as if her emotions had been tumbling over one another all day, and her brain had been running, trying to catch up with them. She had been impatient, and happy, and worried, and excited, and now she was tired and very disappointed.

"It's all Rodney's fault," she said. "If he hadn't told — " She stopped when she saw her mother's eyes laughing at her. Then she remembered the other secret, the one *she* hadn't been able to keep, and she laughed with her mother.

Loritha laughed, too, and a loud yawn escaped. "Oh, excuse me!" she said.

She and Koya didn't protest when their mother said it was time for bed.

"Tomorrow night we'll have a chance to really talk," Koya said to Delbert.

"Hope so, Cuz," Delbert answered.

Sixteen

The picture in the newspaper was huge, almost half the size of the page. It was just their faces, turned to the right, hers a little below his. DEL AND SHERITA, MAKIN' A HOME FOR THE HOMELESS. It was the headline on the front page of the Arts Section.

The article, almost two pages long, was all about the young performers whose record, *Makin' a Home*, had surprised the industry with its fast climb up the charts. It told how Del had started performing as a child, at weddings and recitals, and how he and Sherita had met in high school and formed a group of their own.

It also told how heartbroken they had been two years ago when their first album had been snatched off the market after only a few months. The record company didn't think it was selling fast enough.

Delbert had gone to live with his grandparents when he was in high school, the article said. It didn't mention the reason. Koya knew Delbert would never talk to a reporter about that.

Koya read the article before she went to school Thursday morning, and when she got there, everybody was talking about it. Dr. Hanley had posted a copy on the bulletin board outside her office.

By nine-fifty, the whole school was seated in the auditorium, talking quietly. Koya kept looking back, watching the door. Her mother had kept the car today so that she could bring Delbert to school, and when Koya saw her mother come in and take a seat in the back of the room, she knew Delbert was in the principal's office.

At exactly ten o'clock, there was a burst of applause as Delbert, in a light-blue sweatsuit and white sneakers, walked onto the stage with Dr. Hanley and a little girl from the third grade. Delbert and the girl took seats on the stage.

Dr. Hanley went to the microphone. In her usual way, she said a lot in a few words.

"Welcome, Delbert 'Del' DeLaney. It's an honor to have you with us."

Then, the girl read a short paper about when and where Delbert was born, and how much everybody at Barnett School loved him and his music.

Then it was Delbert's turn.

"I love music, too," he said. "I need it the way I need food. Sometimes when I listen to quiet music, I can feel myself breathing it in and becoming a stronger person."

He asked the children how music made them feel.

"Fast music makes me want to do somersaults," a kindergarten boy said.

"Gives you energy, huh?" Delbert said.

"Yeah," the boy said, happy that Delbert understood. "It gives me *en-der-gy*."

The smiles in the room could almost be heard.

"Music makes me sad, sometimes." It was a girl from fourth grade.

"It makes me happy." A boy.

"It makes me feel like singing." A girl.

"You are all so beautiful," Delbert said, "*you* make *me* feel like singing. And it's a good thing, too," he added, laughing a little, "since that's what I had planned to do for you today."

He said he was going to sing three songs. "Last night," he said, "when I was thinking about what I might do, I decided to sing *a cappella*. Who knows what *a cappella* means?"

A boy said it meant just singing, without a

piano or horns or anything. Delbert said that was right.

"The song I'm going to sing first," he said, "is very special to me. When I wrote this song, I tried to write the sound of my mother's voice. My mother didn't have a great singing voice, but her speaking voice was like soft music with lots of highs and lows. She would say, 'Delbert, *Junior*, I don't want you to do that any*more*.' "

Koya remembered her aunt saying those words, starting low on "Delbert," a little higher on "Junior," then going up the scale to "more."

The children laughed at Delbert's imitation. He let the laughter end, and then he said, "When I was sixteen years old, my parents died in a fire."

The room got very quiet.

"And after that," Delbert continued, "I didn't want to play music anymore, or even listen to it. But the rest of my family, my grandparents, aunts and uncles and cousins, gave me so much love, that after a while, I became myself again. If they hadn't done that, I wouldn't be here to sing for you today."

He told the children that the best way to listen to music was to listen all the way through and not to applaud until every bit of the sound had faded away. And then he sang, and Koya thought it was the most beautiful song she had ever heard.

She could hear her aunt's voice in it. It was soft and slow and had notes that Delbert held a long time, notes going from low to high and back again. The very last note, he held and held, and Koya could see his mouth changing shape, making the sound of the note change. Then it got softer and softer until it faded away and there was no more sound.

For a moment, there was absolute silence, as if it, too, were a part of the music. And then the audience broke the silence with applause. Two of the teachers stood up, and then everybody stood up and applauded for a long time.

Then Delbert taught the children how to sing a new song that Sherita had written, called "Sitting on the Moon," about someone looking down from the sky, seeing the things that were happening all over the world. After that, Delbert said that he was going to sing "Makin' a Home."

"If you know the words," he said, "sing along with me, and I'm inviting you to clap to the beat on this song. That's different from applause. Clapping to the beat is part of the music, it's keeping the rhythm. Okay, come on." He began to clap. "One and two and . . ."

Almost all of the children knew the words, and so did some of the teachers, and even Dr. Hanley was singing and clapping.

Makin' a home in this world
Makin' a place in this world for myself
In this sweet, sweet world
This funny world
This hurtin' world
I'm makin' a home . . .

Delbert took the microphone off its stand and walked back and forth across the stage to the beat of the music. Children were bouncing in their seats. Sound was bouncing off the walls. The room was rocking.

Makin' a home for myself
Makin' a place
Stakin' a place
Takin' my space
I'm makin' a home
Makin' a home
Makin' a home
Makin' a home . . .

Rodney came toward the stage, carrying the picture he had drawn. He wouldn't look at Delbert. He kept his eyes down, even when Delbert handed him the microphone, and Koya knew he was ashamed about telling Delbert's secret. It wasn't until Delbert patted his shoulder that he finally looked up and smiled.

"Brother Del," he said, "this drawing is just a small, tangible token of something we can't really express. How much we love you and how much we appreciate your coming to visit us."

He held the drawing up so everybody could see it. It was Delbert's face, done in charcoal. His head was back and his eyes were closed. It was from a still moment, and Koya knew which song he had been singing.

"Man!" Delbert almost whispered into the mike. "Man, this is something." His voice sounded funny. "You drew this?" he asked Rodney.

"It's not very good," Rodney said. "I had to do it fast."

"It's unbelievable!" Delbert said.

He turned to the audience. "Thank you for this very, very special gift and for being your wonderful, beautiful selves. Take good care of yourselves, now. A lot of people care about you. I love you."

He raised his arm and waved, but didn't smile. He looked as if he hated to leave. Koya snapped a picture of him with her mind, so that she could look at it again when she got home.

Seventeen

"Ma!" Loritha called as she and Koya entered the house.

"In here," Ms. DeLaney called back, from the study.

"Wasn't Delbert, Jr., *some-thinng*!" Koya said.

Her mother was going through some papers. "He was great!" she said. "Nobody could sit still. Not even that teacher . . . what's his name? . . . the one who's always so stiff?"

"Mr. Young," Loritha said.

"Yes, that's the one," her mother said. "He was moving his shoulders. Not much, just an inch to the left and an inch to the right, but he was moving."

"Where's Delbert, Jr.?" Loritha asked.

"I dropped him at the hotel after we left the school," her mother said.

"What time is he coming back?" Koya asked.

"Uh, Koya . . ." Ms. DeLaney said, and Koya knew something was wrong. That was the only time her mother ever began a sentence with "Uh."

"What's wrong?" Koya asked.

"Well, he's going to be so busy," her mother said, "now that Sherita and the band are here. They've got some rehearsing to do, and he's got to check the sound system at the theater — you know how particular he is about that, and . . ."

Loritha was looking at her mother, not saying anything.

"But he's got to sleep somewhere," Koya said.

"Well . . ."

"He's not coming back, is he?" Koya asked. "Because of what happened last night?"

"Well, you know," her mother said, "the shrubbery, and the disturbance to the neighborhood, and all. He thought it would be better if he didn't stay here. But he left our tickets. We'll be down front, fifth row, and he's giving our names to the guards so we can go backstage after the performance. And he told me to tell you and Ritha that he's going to sing his mother's song, and that'll be just for you."

"We didn't get to really talk," Loritha said quietly.

"That's not fair," Koya said. Her voice was shaking. "All those people . . . what they did, that's not fair!"

"Koya . . ." her mother said, but Koya pulled away from her mother's hand and ran upstairs. She closed the door of her room and lay on the bed, crying softly, until she fell asleep. And then she dreamed.

She dreamed that she lived in a house with many rooms. The house was crowded with people who pushed her and screamed at her, trying to awaken the monster that slept under her skin. The monster began to squirm. It struggled to unfold itself and get free, but the more it struggled, the harder she worked to keep it imprisoned.

She wrapped her arms around herself to keep the monster from escaping, stretching her arms so that they went around and around her body hundreds of times in tight, overlapping circles. Her heart hurt from the squeezing. Her bones cracked. Then her lungs, too full of air, fell to dust, and she disappeared. Only the monster was left.

It wore a mask of Koya's face. It had fists that were larger than its head. Unfolded, it stood taller than the rooms, and the ceilings had to rise to make space as it crashed its huge body from room to room, smashing walls and furniture and people, as if they were all the same thing. And even after everything had been destroyed, the monster continued to swing its arms in all directions, pounding the air with its huge fists, as Koya's dream faded away.

She slept a while longer, and by the time her father woke her up for dinner, she had forgotten the dream.

"Feeling better?" her father asked.

She answered yes, but it wasn't true. She felt worse than she had before, but she didn't know why.

Eighteen

Friday night, and the large theater was filling up. While their parents chatted, Koya and Loritha sat turned partially around in their seats, looking back to watch the crowd pouring in.

The teenagers were a fashion show in high heels and velvet, sneakers and jeans, and witty, printed T-shirts. And there were enough gigantic earrings swaying in the theater, Koya thought, to start a tornado. The teenagers waved excitedly at each other across the theater, and Koya knew just how they felt. She had seen Angie and her father coming in, and she and Angie had waved exactly like that, as if they hadn't seen each other for years. It meant, "We're here! And something great is about to happen!"

Koya hoped the music would not be too loud.

She knew her father had in his pocket four sets of earplugs he had bought a few months ago, after they had been to a show where the music was so loud it made Koya's stomach rumble.

"I am not giving you permission to lose your hearing at these shows," Mr. DeLaney had said sternly when Koya and Loritha pouted. "Use the earplugs, or we don't go."

Koya and Loritha had not gone to a show since, preferring to stay home rather than be the only people at the shows with pink balls sticking out of their ears.

The lights in the theater began to dim gradually, and so did the voices, until the whole room was very dark and very quiet. The curtains opened slowly, and there was the band, standing as if a magician had frozen them in the act of playing — the drummer holding one stick on the drum, the other one poised high above it, the guitarist and the bass player bending to their instruments, their fingers near, but not touching, the strings.

There was a long moment of silence. Koya could feel the excitement building. Then the drummer brought the stick down, moving it in slow motion toward the drum. Finally, he touched the drum, barely touched it, and the music began. The audience was yelling louder than the music.

Delbert and Sherita ran onto the stage from opposite entrances, he in black pants and shirt and a shiny red, open vest, and she in red silk tunic and pants. Delbert went to the piano on his side of the stage and Sherita went to the organ on her side. They played standing up, facing each other, and the whole group moved their bodies in rhythm with the music.

The audience got their hands going, hitting the beat on their thighs, on their chairs, in the air. It was a fast piece, one they all knew from the album. There were no words, just places where Delbert and Sherita hummed. The audience hummed along.

The music was not too loud. Koya leaned across her mother, caught her father's eye, and grinned. She knew he could read her mind. "No earplugs!"

The group performed for almost two hours. Delbert and Sherita sang, sometimes separately, sometimes together. They played piano and organ, played trumpet and saxophone, played with and without the band. They didn't really dance, but they had some bad moves.

Delbert sang a whirlwind solo with only the bass behind him. It sounded as if he and the bass were chasing each other. Sherita sang a slow, soft song with the guitar, and then she played a mellow saxophone solo that made the audience applaud at all the wrong times, drowning out the sweet music.

Koya wished Delbert would tell them what he had told the children at her school. She wanted to hear all of the music. She didn't want to miss one note.

"Makin' a Home!" Sherita shouted it into the mike. The audience roared and stood up. They rocked and clapped and sang until the song was over. They applauded so long that the group played the whole song again.

Then, Delbert said it was time to say good night. He said he and Sherita were going to close with a song he had written about his mother's voice. In her imagination, Koya left the theater and went to sit alone in a peaceful place.

Delbert and Sherita sang *a cappella*, mostly in harmony, but sometimes coming together on the same notes. Their voices followed Koya to her special place. Sherita hit a clear, high note and held it. But it was shattered, overpowered, by the sound of many hands being smacked together. Koya felt as if she had been punched in the stomach.

She began to feel squirmy inside, and a part of her dream flashed through her mind. She tried to ignore it and concentrate on the music. But again and again, when the music was most beautiful, it was interrupted. And when the last note was being sung, and Delbert and Sherita were holding the note for a long, long time, there was a rush of noise. People clapped and stamped their feet and shouted, "Sing it! Sing it!"

Koya could see the singers' mouths moving, changing shape, but she couldn't hear them singing. She could only hear noise. She wanted to cry, not because she was disappointed or hurt or sad, but because she was *mad.* She was good and mad, and she didn't care. She wanted to hit somcbody. Shc breathed hard to keep from sobbing.

And then the curtains closed, and the group was gone, and the crowd was rushing toward the stage, filling the aisles so that Koya and her family couldn't leave their seats. They were blocked on both sides.

"Excuse me, excuse me," Koya said. She wanted to get backstage and hug Delbert and cry. She tried to squeeze through, but couldn't move an inch. "*Excuse me!*" she said louder, but the crowd was still pushing forward.

Koya felt something explode inside her, and she not only wanted to hit *some*body, she wanted to hit *every*body. The next thing she knew she was standing on her chair, waving her arms wildly in the air.

"Get out of my way!" she yelled. She knew her face was ugly, and she didn't care. It felt so good, she yelled again. "Get out of my way!"

Her family was staring at her. The people near her looked at her as if she were crazy and began to back away. Her mother held her waist and Loritha sat down hard on the edge of the chair to keep it from flipping up.

Koya saw the guards who had been in a line in front of the stage pushing through the crowd, coming to arrest her. She decided to yell one more time before they took her off to jail.

She waved her arms again. *"I said get out of my waaaay!"* She yelled as loud as she could, although there was no longer anyone anywhere near her. One of the guards took her arm and helped her down. "Come on," he said, laughing. "Your cousin sent us to get you."

"Huh?" Koya said. She had almost forgotten why she was yelling.

Two guards escorted them backstage, and there was a lot of hugging and shaking hands with the band and Sherita. Then Koya's father shook her hand. She started to laugh at his mistake, but he said, "Congratulations." And she knew what he meant.

She went over to Loritha and they hugged for the first time in a long time.

Nineteen

Koya wasn't sleepy. She had her pajamas on, but she wasn't ready to go to bed. She had so much to think about, the show and everything. And she had a new joke to work on for the talent show.

She sat at her desk and wrote the joke on a sheet of paper, working on it until she had it just right before she copied it into her notebook. Then she stood in front of the mirror to practice the joke. She looked hard at her reflection. It was exactly the same as it had been early that day. Anger hadn't left a single mark on her face, as she had thought it surely would.

After she got in bed, she thought about the show and Delbert's visit. On the whole, it hadn't turned out too badly. Delbert had told them, before he said good-bye, that he would be sneaking back into town soon, to spend some time with them. Just them.

She looked at the clock on her dresser. It was getting late, and she needed to go to sleep. She had two important things to do in the morning.

One was the talent show. That wouldn't be too hard. If she remembered to watch her mother in the audience, she wouldn't have stage fright. She knew her mother would laugh at her jokes. The other thing she had to do would be hard. She hoped she could make herself do it.

Her mother was the only one eating when she came down the next morning. Her father had gone out, and Loritha was still in bed.

"Want some hash browns?" her mother asked, pointing to the stove with her fork. Then she noticed the scowl on Koya's face. "What's wrong, Koya?" she asked.

"I'm mad," Koya said, sitting down at the table. There was fire in her eyes.

"What happened?" her mother asked, anxiously. "What's the matter?"

"I'm mad with Dawn for what she did to Ritha," Koya said. "And soon as I get to school, I'm going to walk right up to her and slap her face!"

"Koya, I don't think — "

"I'm going to do it, Ma!" Koya said. "And then I'm going to see Dr. Hanley and tell her that Dawn ought to be kicked out of school for that."

Her mother's eyes widened. "Uh, honey," she said, "your father and I . . . that's not what we meant. . . ."

Koya couldn't hold the scowl any longer. She burst into laughter, hitting the table several times, fast.

"Koya!" her mother said, starting to laugh, too.

"Well, you told me to get mad, Ma!" Koya said. She could hardly talk for laughing.

"Okay, you got me," her mother said, squeezing the words out between gasps of laughter, "but just remember, payback is coming. You'd better watch out."

When they finished laughing, Koya went into the living room and stood beside the phone, not touching it. Now she had to do the hard thing. She didn't know what she was going to say. She didn't really want to say anything. She wasn't a bit angry.

She put her hand on the phone, then took it back and turned to walk away. But then, she remembered Loritha's face and the pain she had seen on it. Dawn had put it there. The memory hurt Koya now. She let herself inhale the anger slowly. Nobody could treat her sister like that. Not even her best friend. She picked up the phone.

"Dawn?" she said when Dawn answered.

"Hi, Koya," Dawn said. She sounded happy to hear from her.

"Hi, nothing!" Koya said. "I don't like what you did to my sister."

"Koya, I — "

"Don't say you called her," Koya said, "because you didn't. Talking about you dreamed a trick. You didn't dream it, you thought it up just to be mean."

Dawn didn't know what to say, and Koya let her suffer in the silence. Neither of them spoke. After a long moment, Dawn said softly, "I was jealous, Koya. I'm sorry."

"You want to be friends with us or not?" Koya asked.

"Yes! I do!" Dawn said. "I miss you and Ritha."

"Well, you have to promise not to do anything like that anymore," Koya said.

"I promise!"

"And you have to apologize to Ritha," Koya said.

"I'll do it this morning," Dawn said. "Soon as I get to school."

"Okay, then," Koya said. "See you later."

Koya started to hang up, but she heard Dawn's intake of breath.

"What?" Koya asked.

"So, are we friends now?"

"*After* you apologize," Koya said. She hung up.

Twenty

The double-dutch team, looking good in their uniforms, walked proudly, in single file, down the aisle of the auditorium. Dawn, carrying the trophy, was first in line, and Loritha was right behind her. Koya, seated in the first row with the rest of the performers, watched them, wondering if things had gone the way she had hoped.

The team walked up on the stage and sat in the chairs that had been placed there for them. Loritha and Dawn were seated side by side, and while the students were performing, Koya kept studying her sister's face, but she couldn't tell what Loritha was feeling.

Then, while the boy Mr. Fillmore had introduced as the next Count Basie was standing beside the piano, taking his bows, Koya saw the sign she had been looking for. Loritha's shoulder was resting against Dawn's. And Koya knew for sure that her sister and her best friend were friends again.

". . . and here she is," Mr. Fillmore was saying, "a new comic on the rise, Miss Koya DeLaney!"

Koya stood up and walked toward the stage. Her mother's black pants, rolled up at the bottom, bagged on her, just the way she had wanted them to. And her father's jacket, too. His gray felt hat just missed covering her eyes. She looked a mess.

She wished Mr. Fillmore hadn't introduced her like that, a comic on the rise. While she was walking, she imagined herself rising slowly toward the ceiling, over the heads of the audience. It was too funny! But the last thing she wanted to do was have a laughing fit. She fought the laughter and won.

"Hey, y'all," she said to the audience, "let me ask you something. Have y'all heard about the new music lovers?"

She watched the faces in the audience. They were listening. She had caught their attention.

"You don't know about 'em, yet?" Koya asked. "Well, let me tell you. Those people, they love music *soooo* much, they can't *wait* to drown it out. Every night, they go around to all the places where folks are listening to music the old-fashioned way, and they show 'em how *real* music lovers act. They don't just sit there and listen. Naw! When the music gets good, they start to clapping . . ."

She clapped as loud as she could, spreading her arms wide apart, then smacking her hands together.

The audience began to laugh.

". . . and stomping . . ."

Koya stomped with first one foot, then the other. Her mother's pants were flapping around her legs. People were really laughing, now. She lifted her knees high, coming down hard and getting faster and faster.

". . . and calling hogs. Sooo*weeee*! Soo! Soo! Soo! Soo!"

She knew she had them. She loved watching them, seeing the happiness in their faces, feeling the laughter rolling toward her in waves and surrounding her. She loved it. She cupped her hands around her mouth.

"Sooo*weeee*!" she called. "Sooo*weeee! . . .* Sooo*weeeeee! . . .*"

About the Author

ELOISE GREENFIELD is the award-winning author of more than twenty books for young readers, ranging from poetry and picture books to fiction and biography. Her works include *Honey, I Love*; *Grandpa's Face*; and *Under the Sunday Tree* — all ALA Notable Books; *Africa Dream*, winner of the Coretta Scott King Award; *Sister*, which received a *New York Times* Outstanding Book Award; and *Rosa Parks*, which received the Carter G. Woodson Award. In a more unusual honor, the students at P.S. 268 in Brooklyn have named their library after her.

Ms. Greenfield is a member of the African American Writer's Guild and lives in Washington, D.C. She has taught creative writing to children as an artist-in-education for the D.C. Commission on the Arts and Humanities.